Black

at the

Ballot Box

Mrs Capper's Casebook #3

David W Robinson

Prologue

Good afternoon and welcome to Christine Capper's Comings & Goings, your weekly look at what's been happening in and around Haxford, sponsored today by Sandra's Snacky, the heart of good food at Haxford Mill, where the meals are hot but won't burn a hole in your pocket.

Don't you think it would be wonderful if we could see into the future? Perhaps not. If everyone knew which lottery numbers were going to come out on any given Saturday, the jackpot would be less than you actually pay for your tickets.

On the other hand, there are those circumstances where if you could see the future, it would be a spectacular advantage, and that was true of the case I took on early in May. Had I known what was going to happen, I would have turned the client down on the spot.

I'm going to take you back to the days leading up to the by-election created by the untimely death of our long-time MP, Cyril Utteridge, a man who became almost a legend in the town having served the interests of his constituents for over twenty years.

Like everyone else, Dennis and I were plagued

by canvassers from the various parties putting up candidates and also like everyone else, we were getting tired of it. So much so that the lady who rang my doorbell two weeks before polling day faced the rough edge of my tongue.

As it happened, I had her reasons for calling all wrong, and now that it's all public knowledge, and with her agreement, I can tell you the full story, but I have to warn you that it is not a pretty tale.

Chapter One

British weather. I know that meteorology isn't a precise science, and yet for those of us who remember Wincey Willis and Michael Fish, 21st century computer modelling has done wonders, but even so it's still not much better than intelligent guesswork.

There was one thing I could guarantee with the weather. Because Haxford sat in a valley, when it rained the outlying areas, such as the upper end of Moor Road where we lived, were witness to torrents of water running down to town as if they were trying to emulate Niagara. And the water got there a lot faster than the local buses. Notwithstanding that, flooding in the town centre was rare. Dennis said it had something to do with the porous nature of the land around us, aided by the river Hax which ran through the town. He could be right, though to be honest, what Dennis knows about porous bedrock and subterranean water drainage could probably be written on a Post-It note and still leave room for his name and address. And at no point in its meandering journey was the Hax wide enough or deep enough to carry all that water away. If you took a kayak on the Hax, you'd spend most your time wading through a few inches of water and carrying your canoe. Where anyone in the town's history found the audacity to describe it as a river, I do not know.

I have to say that during that wet, May week, when we were subject to days of non-stop, heavy rain, it had one big advantage. It kept the election canvassers away from the door.

Politics was one of those areas that never interested me, and in that respect I was in good company. Dennis had no time for them no matter what party flag they flew. He voted (I think). It would be more accurate to say that I made him go to the polling station on the grounds that many people in history had fought and sometimes died for the right to a democratic vote, but what he actually put on the ballot paper, was anyone's guess. For all I knew he could have drawn a small diagram of an engine block and crankshaft. I always voted the same way (no I'm not going to tell you which way) and while I wouldn't have recognised the late Cyril Utterridge if I bumped into him on the High Street, I knew that he had been our MP for many years.

Many of our neighbours put up party leaflets in the windows, hoping to deter the opposition canvassers (without success). Dennis put a notice in our window. "If you're selling summat or chasing voats (sic) and you don't like being told to get stuffed, don't bother knocking." It didn't stay there long. The moment I saw it, I took it down. Not that I disagreed with the sentiments, but I was not about to give Fred and Barbara Timmins, our next door neighbours, the opportunity to gossip about Dennis's grumpiness… or his spelling.

Perhaps I should have left the notice there. With a by-election looming, we were plagued with party workers campaigning for anything and everything from rejoin the Common Market (I believe it was someone who had never updated his/her thinking from the sixties or early seventies) to free Class A drugs on the NHS, hang all shoplifters and be done with it, to murder is necessary to keep the population at sensible levels. Somewhere in between these sometimes idiotic extremes were the mainstream parties spouting economic mumbo-jumbo which neither of us could understand and about which neither of us really cared.

With two weeks to go to polling day, I was glad of the rain. It was good for the garden, helped ensure the reservoirs were full and able to cope with the promised (and as yet, mythical) heatwave and drought we were expecting, and it gave us some peace from the politicos.

Cappy the Cat didn't care for the near biblical deluge. Cats don't, do they? He wanted to go out on that first morning so I opened the conservatory door for him. He took one look and one sniff at the rain and changed his mind. Then he had this gem of an idea. It occurred to him that it was raining at the back of the house so the simple solution was to go out at the front instead. I opened the front door and of course, it was raining there, too. He gave me a look of absolute disgust as if asking how I'd managed to arrange that, then skulked off back to his basket in the front room.

The rain gave Dennis more than his fair share of problems too. He was a top flight auto-engineer but he was inundated with drivers who didn't know how to make their wipers swish back and forth as they're meant to do, rather than swishing back and forth and turning circles into the bargain. He had other motorists begging him to stop the water leaking through the bottom end of the windscreen, and at least one customer who could not understand why there was a pool of water in the well of the driver's seat. According to Dennis, it was leaking in through the bodywork at the point where the clutch and brake cables came through from the engine compartment.

"I'm making a lot of money," he grumbled, "but I didn't train to be a mechanic to faff about with tiddly-fiddly jobs like that."

My husband is the paradigm of reliability. No matter what the weather, what the circumstances, how much money he was making, he would moan.

It's one of those areas where we British lead the world, isn't it? And what better way to go for Olympic Gold than to gripe about the weather, the favourite topic of any conversation between two Brits. Meet a British couple in Tenerife and it's 'far too hot', bump into them in Lapland and it's 'much too cold'. I often wondered how they'd cope with the Moon where there was no atmosphere and consequently no weather. They'd probably sit in silence.

It was into such random and pointless thoughts that the sound of the doorbell intruded. For once I was ahead of my game. I had recorded my weekly vlog (this week's topic, the weather. What else?) the previous day, I had completed the minor editing it required, and I was enjoying a morning cup of tea when the door chimed for my attention.

I wasn't expecting anyone and it was too early for the postman. Not that I was expecting anything from him that wouldn't fit through the letter box. A quick check through the front windows revealed a large, white, chauffeur-driven limousine parked at the end of our drive, and a middle aged woman, umbrella raised, standing on the doorstep, wearing a large, blue rosette. I meant she was wearing a large, blue rosette, not our front doorstep. She was another pain in the BTM.

I put on my annoyed face and made my way to the front door. It wasn't really a put on. I was annoyed. I yanked it open and said, "We vote for—"

"Am I talking to Mrs Capstan?"

She couldn't even be bothered to get my name right and that only fuelled my irritation. "Capper. Mrs Capper. Capstan were full strength cigarettes my granddad used to smoke. And I don't vote—"

"I'm Eileen McCrudden, prospective parliamentary candidate for the Conservative party."

"I know who you are," I lied. To be honest, I recognised her, but if pushed, I would never have put a name to the ageing face. "And if you allow me to finish, I was going to say, we don't vote for you. We're Labour." If she had said she was from the Labour Party, I would have told her we voted Conservative.

"No, you don't understand. I got your name and address from someone at Haxford Public Library, and—"

There was only one candidate and in a demonstration of my ability to steal a march on Mrs McCrudden, I said, "Kim Aspinall has no business giving out my address, and I don't care how she and Alden Upley vote. Try next door. I'm sure Fred and Barbara are Tories."

I could see she was losing it, too. Her chin jutting out, her volume increasing told me the tale. "Mrs Capper—"

"Don't take that tone with me. Not on my own doorstep."

"Please listen to me. I'm not vote-catching."

That caused me some confusion. If she wasn't vote-catching why was she wearing a pale blue anorak bearing a large, blue rosette, and why was she carrying a load of leaflets in her free hand? The only thing not blue about her was her umbrella, which was a nice, neutral shade of amber. But I still wouldn't vote for her if it were green.

When I put the question to her, she had a ready excuse. "A necessary subterfuge, I'm afraid."

"People round here are not that strong on subterfuge, Mrs McCrudden." It was an understatement. Most people in Haxford wouldn't know what it meant.

"I need your neighbours to think I am chasing votes," she went on, "but in truth, I'm looking for a private investigator, and a young woman at the library gave me your name and number and when I insisted I needed to speak to you personally and in private, she was persuaded to give me your address."

I was right. It had to be Kim. An old friend, she would be cagey, but when she was convinced the query was genuine, she would give way. Even so, it would have been preferable if she'd rung asking whether I was willing to speak to this woman. I put that to Mrs McCrudden, and she readily explained.

"I asked for her discretion. I can't take the risk of anyone else overhearing. Not even my chauffeur."

And she didn't want to take risks? Kim's idea of discretion ended with keeping to herself the number of cream cakes I bought in Warrington's.

Some of the forcefulness had gone from Mrs McCrudden. "Please, Mrs Capper. As I understand it, you're the only serious, sensible private investigator in Haxford."

I was not yet ready to back down. "I'm actually the only private investigator in Haxford. Well, the only one properly trained and licenced. And I don't normally meet potential clients in my home. We usually meet on neutral territory or in the client's home."

Now she was all but pleading. "I can't. Please. I need help but the matter is so sensitive that I daren't discuss it with anyone… except that I have to. Frankly, I'm reluctant to talk to you about it, but I have no choice. I'm desperate."

At last, I relented. "You'd better come in."

She stepped over the threshold, half turned to shake off her umbrella, wiped her feet on the mat and removed her coat, which I hung over the hall radiator. "It'll dry it out," I assured her.

I led her through to the kitchen and into the conservatory, where I invited her to sit while I made tea for us. It was almost inevitable that Cappy the Cat would pay us a visit. He always did when sounds from the kitchen reached his ever-hungry ears. Right on cue, he turned up, but when he realised I wasn't putting him a feed down, he disappeared into the conservatory to check out our visitor, and by the time I joined them, he was purring contentedly on her lap. Little traitor. Sucking up to newcomers in the hope that they might offer him titbits. And it's not as if he would even vote for her.

"What a delightful cat," Eileen said, accepting a cup of tea from me.

"His name is Cappy the Cat and normally, he's anything but friendly."

"Cappy the Cat? Strange name."

"Necessary," I said. "My husband, Dennis Capper is known as Cappy to all his friends. When we christened the cat, we gave him the same name, but we had to add the words, 'the cat' to avoid confusion. It would sound a bit odd if I was telling friends how Cappy likes to chase a strand of wool across the carpet." I settled into an armchair opposite her and placed my cup and saucer on the occasional table between us. "So, Mrs McCrudden, let me lay out my terms before we go any further."

"It doesn't matter what you charge, Mrs Capper, I'll pay it."

"And if I charge a thousand pounds an hour?"

Her eyes popped and for one frightening moment, I thought she would drop the cup and saucer, and they were part of my best dinner service.

"It's all right. I don't charge anything of the kind." My usual charges were twenty pounds an hour plus expenses, which was quite cheap as PIs go, but I recalled the white limousine at the gate, and adjusted my thinking accordingly. "I charge fifty pounds an hour plus any out of pocket expenses."

She persuaded Cappy the Cat to get off her lap, reached forward and put her cup and saucer on the table, much to my relief. "Ms Aspinall at the library seemed to think it was twenty pounds an hour."

Typical politician. She knew the price of everything, the value of nothing. "That's mates' rate," I lied, "but like everything else in the country my prices have had to go up. I blame Brexit, but let's not get into politics. I was talking about my terms. I don't do criminal cases, I don't do confrontation. Most of the time, I concentrate on divorce evidence and tracing missing persons."

I threw in the phrase 'most of the time' to give the impression that I was busy, busy, busy, but I usually averaged three or four cases per year, although I saw no reason why she should be party to that information.

"Finally," I concluded, "it's my decision whether I take the case or not."

"Those terms are acceptable. A little pricey, but to be brutally honest, I have no choice."

Pricey? Most professional investigators charged at least twice the amount I was quoting. Was this another politician who chose not live in the real world? I decided it was another debate I didn't want to get into. "Fine. So what seems to be the problem?"

"I'm being blackmailed."

Chapter Two

"Go to the police."

"I can't. It's—"

I cut her off before she could say any more. "Mrs McCrudden, blackmail, extortion, call it what you like, is a criminal offence, and it's a matter for the police. As a Conservative, you should be aware of that. I mean you're all members of the flog 'em and hang 'em brigade, aren't you?"

She quivered with indignation. "I have to say, Mrs Capper, you don't go out of your way to make your clients feel comfortable, do you?"

"I'm simply being honest."

"Well, you're mistaken. As it happens, I'm a supporter of penal reform and I have always stood against the death penalty and all forms of corporal punishment. And I have gone on record as anti-Brexit, and I'm also opposed to—"

"Yes, yes." I interrupted before she could get into the detail of her manifesto. "I said, let's forget politics. Politicians in general are not my favourite people because they don't deal in something which I hold sacred: the truth, plain speaking, telling it like it is." I leaned forward to stress my point. "I'm exactly the opposite, and I'm telling you that blackmail is a criminal offence, and if you fail to report it, you are just as guilty."

She breathed out a heavy sigh and I was sure I saw the sparkle of tears in her eyes. Time to back off, Capper, I thought.

"I'm sorry to be so blunt, but I was a police officer for many years, and I know the law."

Another slight exaggeration on my part. I was a police officer, Capper the Copper, they used to call me, but I only did eight years and I gave it up when my son (also a police officer these days) was born. I did know the law, but I knew it back in the mid-to-late eighties. Even so, I was certain that the rules on blackmail hadn't changed. It was still an offence.

"Your friend, Ms Aspinall told me of your history with the police. Indeed, that was one of the reasons she recommended you when I asked for a private investigator. And I understand what you're saying, Mrs Capper, but as yet, you don't know what the blackmailer is using to threaten me, nor what his demands are. I need someone to unmask him and help me persuade him to back off. Please. I'm not used to begging but I am begging you for help."

I could feel my resolve weakening. It was as if she knew me, as if the magic words 'you don't know what he's using to threaten me' would draw me in. I'm not by nature a gossip… well, no worse than anyone else in Haxford, which on reflection was perhaps not the best recommendation, but if I was about to become privy to the dirty dealings of a politician, it was almost too big a temptation to resist.

Correction. Not almost. It was too attractive to

resist as I realised when I heard myself saying, "I will need all the details, no matter how dirty, demeaning or potentially illegal." I held up a hand as she opened her mouth to protest again. "It's not negotiable, Mrs McCrudden. I cannot tackle your problem without knowing everything, and if you're not willing to take me into your confidence, then I can't take the case. You have my assurance that whatever you say to me will remain confidential. No one else will hear anything of it."

Other than Dennis, I thought, but even he'd only get to hear about it if and when she became the MP she so desperately wanted to be. Besides, telling Dennis anything was safe enough. Unless I was complaining about my tappets tapping or big ends ending, he wouldn't listen. If I told him that Barbara and Fred Timmins had committed armed robbery, his interest would end with the vehicle they used for the getaway.

Opposite me, Eileen sipped her tea and appeared uncomfortable, which was strange. I found our conservatory furniture, two armchairs and a two-seater settee comfortable enough for my afternoon zizz, and Cappy the Cat had never complained… well, no more than the occasional hiss and spat.

"Very well. But I must have your assurance that you will not breathe a word to another living soul."

Having already told her that confidentiality was assured, I was tempted to ask, 'how about dead souls?' but I didn't. Instead, I replied, "I've already given you such assurance."

"Very good. In that case…"

She trailed off and looked more uncomfortable.

"Would you like me to get you a couple of cushions?" I asked. "Only those seats can get a bit hard on the old BTM after a time."

"No, no. I'm fine. I'm just wondering where to begin."

Annoyed with myself at having misinterpreted her body language, I asked, "Have you ever seen The Sound of Music?"

"Of course?"

"Then take Julie Andrews's advice and start at the beginning." At this point, I realised I hadn't been half enough nosy. I knew next to nothing about her. "Or alternatively, let me ask you a couple of questions. First, are you a Haxforder?"

"Yes. I was born here in Haxford. The northwest side of town, of course."

Well, she would be, wouldn't she? If you were looking for a des res in Haxford, away from hoi polloi like Dennis and me, you'd try the northwest first.

"I went to York University and eventually settled into teaching in Huddersfield. That's where I met Keith."

"Keith?"

"My husband. He's a good ten years older than me. A successful businessman. Ours has been a happy marriage, Mrs Capper."

"Please call me Christine."

"Thank you. And I'm Eileen."

I smiled an invitation. "Do go on."

"We've been married almost thirty years and we have two wonderful daughters, Hermione and Charlotte. They're both married and settled, and they've presented us with three grandchildren between them. And I assume you've already realised that Keith and I are quite, er, well off, I suppose you would say."

She was right. I had already guessed it from the limousine currently blocking access to our drive. In Haxford, you don't show up in something like that unless you're well-heeled, have a loaded lover or you've stolen it. I didn't voice the thought, but continued to listen.

"Ten years ago, maybe a little longer, I did something very foolish. I became involved with a younger man."

I think my ears pricked up like Cappy the Cat's. I must have reacted somehow because that same moggie perked up and gave me a malevolent stare. It caused me to wonder whether he had taught himself to understand words like 'involved with a younger man'. But in that case, why would he be looking at me? I'd never even so much as looked at another man in all the years Dennis and I had been together. All right, I had looked, I had indulged in the odd daydream. Don't we all? But that's as far as it went and it did not justify Cappy the Cat's glaring accusation. Then again, maybe he was just peckish.

"And your husband doesn't know?" The question was aimed at my visitor, not Cappy the Cat, who didn't have a husband. I was trying to take the discussion further.

"That's just it. He does know. He found out quite early on because I told him. I couldn't live with the guilt, you see."

Now that, I couldn't understand. Sure, there were

times when I felt guilty. Like paying fifty pounds for a dress and telling Dennis that it only cost twenty. He didn't know the difference in quality or brand name, and he could go on his way quite happy in his ignorance. Nothing on earth would persuade me to appease my conscience by telling him the truth. Anyway, I viewed the minimal guilt associated with such episodes as a punishment for having spent so much in the first place.

While my thoughts rambled, Eileen was still speaking.

"I called it a mid-like crisis. I was in my forties, my looks and figure were declining, I was no longer attractive, and Keith had never been the most, er, active man. You understand?"

I nodded. When it came to action, I could say the same about Dennis, but I'd never used that as an excuse for straying from the marital straight and narrow.

"I met Wayne Pearson when I attended a two-day course at Lancaster University. It was designed to bring us up to scratch on changes to the national curriculum. Needless to say, attendance was compulsory. He worked in Huddersfield, the same as me. Different schools of course. He was good deal younger than me. Only in his late twenties, perhaps early thirties. We had a few drinks in the hotel bar, and one thing led to another and... I tell, you Christine, I have never felt such a confusing mixture of shame and excitement. It was almost as if I was reborn, and yet I was the happily married mother of two teenage daughters." She took a moment to bring her turgid emotions under control.

"Our affair lasted less than a month before I brought it to an end. I simply could not live with the guilt. Wayne understood my point of view and we parted as friends. I told my husband about it. He was angry and upset, but as time went on we smoothed over the cracks and since then, I swear to you, I have never been tempted, let alone succumbed to the charms of another man."

I couldn't tell whether she was waiting for approbation or condemnation. I decided that she was expecting a comment but for now my mind was filled with vicarious images of this overweight, middle aged crumblie (surely a good few years older than me) entwined with a young stud.

Realisation dawned, a consequence of putting two and two together and getting four instead of half a dozen, and I snapped out of my prurient reverie. "Until now? You're in the political spotlight and he's seen the opportunity to sting you for a payoff?"

She did not agree. "I very much doubt it. If he's still teaching, he risks his own career, not just mine. And as I said, he was the epitome of understanding when I terminated our relationship. There are, however, aspects of our affair which I haven't told you about."

"Then tell me."

I didn't really want to know what she and her boyfriend got up to. Or did I? I'm only human and the opportunity to ponder what other people considered fun was too good to pass up, but such discussion usually had me crimson... with embarrassment, I hasten to add, not envy. I did not consider myself particularly prudish, but I never did get around to reading Fifty Shades of Grey.

Opposite me, Eileen squirmed with embarrassment. "Oh, I can't. I'm far too ashamed."

For a moment, I wondered what she was talking about and then I remembered I had asked her to tell me about these 'aspects'. I knew this woman would be hard work when I met her on the doorstep. I also knew that when (if) she made it to the House of Commons, she would be a standard, verbose bore, spending a long time telling the tale without getting to the nub of the issue.

"Mrs McCrudden, Eileen, you're asking for my help. I cannot do anything until you get into detail. Believe me, there's nothing you can say that will shock me."

That was another little fabrication. I'm not exactly innocent, but I felt there was a great deal she could tell me. She had the look of a woman who had clocked up more than a few active hours, and there were those practices between consenting adults that I knew little or nothing about, and I didn't really want to know.

She blurted it out. "We used to write lurid love letters to each other. I would tell him what I wanted him to do to me, and he would tell me what he was going to do."

And this was a blessed area of ignorance for me.

I knew this kind of thing went on, but I thought it was limited to young men and women barely out of school. Or still in school, even. Back in my schooldays, we would pass notes around when the teacher's back was turned, but they were things like,

'*I saw you snogging Doggo Stubley last night. Your dinner money every day next week or your dad gets to know.*' These days it would no doubt be text messages, but the principle was the same: simple, childish games of extortion.

I recall writing love letters to Simon Le Bon but even so I was only declaring my adoration, not telling him what I expected of him. Good heavens, I was only about thirteen years old. And Dennis never wrote letters to me. Not that I was troubled by it. Aside from his shocking spelling, his letter would have been more about what he was doing to a Ford Cortina than anything he had planned for me.

My first thought when she admitted it was 'Ugh'. On reflection, at least they weren't taking photographs or videoing the action.

That was another facet of modern life which escaped my understanding. Give me a video of Daniel Craig getting down to business with some woman, and I might just take a peek, purely to study his acting technique, naturally, but the thought of Dennis setting up a camera for our infrequent adventures, would have me running for the spare room, or more likely sending him to the spare room, where he'd stay until he learned his lesson. Not that Dennis would even consider it. Ask him to star in a series of photographs while he stripped down the engine of an Austin Cambridge, and he'd be all for it, but other than that, he would not want to know. He didn't even like having his picture taken when we were on holiday.

Topless sunbathing on the Costa del Sol was one thing (and I didn't do that these days) but I could not imagine any woman entertaining the urge to look at pictures of herself and her boyfriend hard at it, and that included Mrs McCrudden and said boyfriend. According to my estimate, she weighed in at about thirteen stones and had a face that could be described as 'lived in'. Not that any viewer would have seen much of her face on such snaps. She was getting on, true, but I couldn't see her being much more nimble, nubile, or attractive a decade previously. Perhaps my thinking might be unkind … all right, so I was being unkind, but unless the boyfriend was plain and plug ugly, or a simple sex-addict, I couldn't see what attraction she might have held for him on or off camera.

But of course, we were not talking about photographs. We had avoided that level of sordidity… is there such a word? He'd sent her copies of the letters for inclusion in her autobiography, and the only way it made sense was to add a couple of financial demands, although I had to question why it took him ten years to get round to it.

I put the proposition to her, but adjusted it slightly. "Someone has sent you a copy of one or more of these letters along with his demands, and you don't believe it could be Wayne?"

"You're right, but it's definitely not Wayne. That's why I said he would be risking his own livelihood, never mind mine. I think someone has got hold of these letters and is using them in an effort to coerce me. Now you see what the problem is, Christine. I can't go to the police. What with the internet and social media and whatnot, if the police find this person, what's to stop him putting them in the public domain?"

"With the best will in the world, the same applies if I track him down."

"I'm aware of that, but at least you can put him and me in touch and we can negotiate."

It was a naïve idea and it reinforced my determination not to vote for her at the coming by-election. What use was an MP who was so gormless? Scratch that. On those occasions when I watched bits and pieces from Westminster, it applied to most of them.

No matter what assurances the blackmailer gave her – or me – there was no guarantee that he would not make the letters public even after he'd been paid. And if he handed them over, it would mean nothing. They were too easy to scan and store on a home computer.

Still, she seemed determined to get me out there looking for him, so the least I could do was show willing. "I'll need to see the letters, and I need to know how much he's demanding."

"I can't show them to you. I'd be far too embarrassed."

"You're doing it again, Eileen. I'm here to help not judge, and I don't particularly like that kind of, er, prose—" *(But Dennis's mates might so I'd have to be careful to keep them away from him)* "— and I'm not interested in looking at them, but you don't know what they can tell us about the perpetrator." Neither did I, but I knew people who had friends who were in touch with others who could tear the whole thing apart and not only tell you when they were produced but which ballpoint Wayne preferred. "I'll need them, Eileen."

She put her cup and saucer down again. "If it has to be, then it has to be."

"Good. Now tell me how much he's demanding."

"Oh, he hasn't demanded money. He wants me to drop out of the by-election."

Chapter Three

Her announcement fazed me. The guy did not want cash, but her withdrawal, retirement, resignation, whatever you want to call it, from the election? It was a clever ploy and it opened up the suspects from just Wayne and no one else, to Wayne and her opponents in the election, of which I think there were three.

Equally surprising was the notion that she hadn't thought of this herself and approached them. Maybe she had and maybe they had given her the bum's rush. If I assumed that to be the case, how come she hadn't decided to fight back with dirt on them? Maybe she had but couldn't find anything to blackmail them with.

I put on my detective hat. "Tell me something, Eileen. How did you receive these letters? By post?"

"Email. They were images of the letters, large enough to be read clearly. They were backed up by text messages with the photographs attached."

At least I had a start point. But deciding on the way forward needed some thinking and I couldn't think clearly while she was opposite me. "Let me make some fresh tea."

She agreed and as I left for the kitchen, she was

entertaining Cappy the Cat, fussing over him, and he loved it.

While waiting for the kettle to boil, I considered my approach to the investigation. I'd need to find Wayne if at all possible, because he was the first line of attack. Beyond that, I would need to confront the other candidates, and I was less sanguine about that. I would also need to speak to someone about analysing the texts and images to see what, if anything, they could tell us. The most obvious person to give me a lead on likely providers of such services was Lester Grimes, one of Dennis's business partners, but Grimy, as he was known to everyone but me, was incapable of keeping anything, secrets, money, absolutely anything to himself, especially after a busy night in the Engine House pub. He had two ex-wives, which shows just how careless he could be.

As cases went, this was a daunting prospect and I was glad I'd established a charge of fifty a day instead of my usual twenty. She could afford it.

What also occurred to me was the potential for danger. I was under no illusions about modern politicians. They weren't exactly the mafia, and I suspect that while many of them sought election because they felt the need to contribute to the governing of the country, once they got their feet under the Westminster table, they were quite happy to compromise their ambitions in order to keep their snout in the trough, and in this instance, if I challenged them, I would be rocking the boat while it was still on the slipway. Would they react with violence? Possible. Maybe not the mainstream party representatives, but the indies were another matter, and I was certain there was at least one such individual standing in the by-election, a right-winger with extreme views on everything from dealing with the unemployed (compulsory military service) to shipping immigrants back where they came from (Leeds or Manchester in most instances).

I had never played these games, and I wasn't particularly keen now.

Putting aside my possible lines of inquiry, Eileen McCrudden was not the kind of woman I'd invite for morning coffee, but that was the way it was with private investigators. You might not like the clients, but you were duty bound to do your best once you agreed to take the case. And all right, so I didn't like her, but I liked blackmail even less. As a police officer, I'd faced intimidation on many occasions. As a cop, I could call for backup. As a private eye, there was no one. I say no one. There was Simon, my son. As an acting detective constable, that stage of a CID career where the officer was on a trial run, he would pitch in and help if I needed him, and I suspected I might just need him, and there was his sergeant, Mandy Hiscoe, an old friend from way back when. She was heavily pregnant and getting close to her due date, but that wouldn't stop her confronting politicians, the thuggish variety or otherwise.

There were other police officers who might be willing to support me, but Mandy's boss, DI Paddy Quinn was not amongst them. I was sure that he would not tolerate any form of intimidation, but in my case he'd wait until they'd beaten me to a pulp before intervening. Anything to get his own back for embarrassments like the Graveyard Poisoner and the Haxford Wool Fair, two cases where I'd shown him the error of his ways as well as getting to the perpetrator before him.

I made the tea, collected a notebook and pen (which I should have had with me from the start but which I forgot) and tucking them under my arm, picked up the cups and returned to the conservatory, where Cappy the Cat was now sound asleep on Eileen's lap.

"Just brush him off," I advised when I saw her torn between doubt and death over disturbing him so she could take her cup and saucer. "He'll get the message."

"But he's so peaceful."

I tittered. "Try getting him into a pet carrier for a trip to the vet's. He'll take the skin off your hands." I took a sip from my cup and set it down on the table. "Okay, Eileen, I can see your problem, but there are some things I need to spell out to you because, although I'll try my best, this is unlikely to be cut and dried in ten minutes. I will have to speak to people, particularly this Wayne Pearson and your election opponents."

"Oh dear. Is there no alternative?"

"None. They're the most likely suspects." I held up my hand to forestall her inevitable objection. "I know, I know, you said it couldn't be Wayne, but how long is it since you last saw him?"

"I told you. Ten years."

"There's been no contact between you since the affair ended?"

"None at all."

"Do you have a photograph of him?"

"I may have an old one at home. I'm not sure. But I disposed of all such, er, memorabilia when I terminated the, er, affair."

Typical. Bury it as deep as possible. Then again, I had boyfriends before I met Dennis and I didn't save photographs of them, so maybe she had it right. As a faithful wife, I'd never put myself in the position she was in.

I focused on the problem at hand. "Considering you haven't had any contact from him for so long, he could have changed all out of recognition, and if so, when he saw you were standing in the by-election, he may have decided to try and cash in."

"I'd be very disappointed in him." She shooed Cappy the Cat from her lap. He gave her a familiar, 'how dare you' scowl and plodded off to the front room, leaving her to pick up her tea. "You mentioned my election opponents?"

"I'm speaking as an observer, and the way I see it, politics can be a dirty game. If they've got hold of this material, no matter how or where from, it makes you an easy target and even though they say no one will hear anything if you choose to follow their instructions, I wouldn't put it past them to drop enough hints to the press in an effort to destabilise the candidate who replaces you in the election."

She blanched, the cup and saucer shook, and once again I worried about my best dinner service.

"I'm ruined. My political career is in tatters before it's even begun."

I felt like telling her she was a no-hoper anyway.

Haxford had long been a Labour stronghold. Even in the General Election when voters avoided Labour like the entire party was carrying coronavirus, Haxford still returned Cyril Underwood. The bald truth, acquainting her with reality, was not the best approach with a woman like this. She needed more delicate handling. Besides, I was disgusted at the perpetrator. Whether I agreed or not with Eileen McCrudden's policies (and I didn't know because I didn't know what they were) it was an absolute no-no to try to take advantage of her in this way.

Perhaps encouragement and common sense would work. "You know, Eileen, I have to say that the best way to avoid blackmail and blackmail*ers* is to be up front about whatever is in your past. Tell the world what happened, but tell it your way. You were young and foolish, these things happen, you've had time to realise the error of your ways, your husband has forgiven you, and you are now the model wife with different values to that woman all those years ago."

In better control of herself, she sipped tea. "To be frank, Christine, I don't give a damn what other people might think, and I give even less of a damn who knows about it. My concern is the danger of this material coming into the public domain. If even one of these letters turns up on the internet, I'll be forever known as the Call Girl of the Commons."

I had to suppress a laugh. I hadn't heard the words 'call girl' for many a year and if by some remote fluke she did win the election, the Great British social media cynics would be sure to come up with much stronger, more revolting epithets.

"We don't know who the blackmailer is," I stressed in an effort to bring the discussion back on track, "and we need to find out. The only way I can do that is to confront and question the likely suspects. I have to start with your election opponents and Wayne Pearson. Remember, my discretion is assured." Given the subject matter of our debate, it sounded like I was offering to send her something in a plain brown wrapper. "Did you say your husband is aware of the affair?"

"He is, but you don't seriously imagine—"

"Of course not," I cut in. "But he might have spoken to someone at some time in the past ten years, and that someone might have put two and two together, found Wayne Pearson and pressured him into handing over the letters. Is your husband – Keith did you say his name was – aware of the blackmail?"

"He is. I told him right away. He also knows that I'm consulting a private detective and he's in complete agreement."

"I will need to speak to him, too."

"I don't see why, but if you feel you must, then do so, but please go easy with him. He has a minor heart condition. Nothing too serious but he's already stressed by this business and I don't want him suffering further. You'll need to ring him in advance to make an appointment. He's a very busy man."

I held up my hands in a gesture of compliance. "Trust me, I shall be the soul of gentility."

A professional private investigator takes notes as she's talking to her client. I was a professional private investigator, but I hadn't bothered with the notes. It was one of those areas where I really needed to get my act together. Trouble was whenever I tried it, my notes usually ended up with irrelevant asides like 'one box of Weetabix' written alongside more important information.

It happened now as I took her husband's business address from her. Longberry reminded me of loganberries, which reminded me of strawberry, which reminded me that we needed a jar of strawberry jam. My note read, *Keith McCrudden Construction, Unit 10 Longberry Trading Estate (strawberry jam)*. It looked bizarre, but I would know what it meant.

"And Wayne Pearson's address?" I asked.

"I haven't the remotest idea," Eileen declared. "As I say, it's ten years since I last saw him, and back then he was living in a council flat in Huddersfield. He's not there now."

This surprised me. "You've been there?"

"The moment I received the email and texts." The thin smile she gave could have been construed as superior or evil. I wasn't sure which. "One does not get through years of teaching teenagers and fighting one's political corner without developing some degree of courage, Christine."

"Of course not. But you insist he's innocent."

"I do, but it was the obvious start point." She lifted her hands and let them fall into her lap. "However, I drew a blank, and I wouldn't know where you should start looking for him."

I'd already made up my mind on that. "I'll start with the electoral roll at the library."

"But he lives in Huddersfield."

"And we have a Huddersfield postcode. You must trust me, Eileen. I know what I'm doing. And right now, I need to get on with what I'm doing. I need a contact number for you, and the moment I have any news, I'll be in touch."

She finished her tea, took my pad and pen, wrote down her phone number and then got to her feet. "I shall wait to hear from you."

"And I'll need you husband's number."

With a whispered 'tsk' she scribbled that down too, and made for the door, but not before I had to ask her to return my pen. That was how Dennis got hold of them and if she was rolling in that much money, she had no business pinching my cheap pens from Benny's Bargain Basement.

Chapter Four

When Eileen left, I stood at the door and watched her limo reverse in, hoping her driver would not hit either of the gateposts because I knew Dennis would blame me. He managed to squeeze the big car between said posts, and pulled away down the street, and with them gone, it was time to get on with the job. She was paying me a lot of money for this gig, and raining or not, I had to show willing.

I shifted to the bedroom and dug out some sensible, private investigator type clothing, an outfit that would look professional, spelling out someone not to mess with. As always, I settled for my dark business suit and a white, opaque blouse, and I was tossing up whether the rain would ruin my best pair of courts when the phone rang.

I was expecting it to be either Dennis, pestering over something and nothing, Kim ringing to tell me she'd spoken to Eileen McCrudden about me, or Eileen herself telling me something she had forgotten to mention, such as the size of her lover's plaything.

In fact, it was none of them. It was a number I thought I should recognise but didn't, and neither did the phone. I made the connection.

"Christine Capper."

"Is that Christine Capper?"

Like the number, I felt I should recognise the voice, but I couldn't place it. "Didn't I just say so?"

"Sure you did, sugar."

One of those calls was it? What was he going to sell me? A new phone which would make sure everyone would hear my name properly?

"Who is this?"

"Your very own Reggie Monk, darlin'."

I knew I should have recognised the voice. Reggie Monk was the voice of Radio Haxford, on air from breakfast time through to about noon every day.

"So what do you want, Reggie?"

"You, my love. I want you."

My irritation-ometer was beginning to rise. "Don't you think my husband might have something to say about that? And don't forget, he services your car. I wouldn't want him to fit some kind of explosive device to your petrol tank."

"Ha-ha-ha. Good old Dennis. How is he?"

"Busy as ever and making a fortune from people like you. Now for the second time, Reggie, I'm as busy as him, so what do you want?"

"I told you. I want you. I put it to the owners and they've agreed."

I was becoming more puzzled than irritated. "You've put what to the owners of what?"

"How would you like a fifteen minute spot once a week on Radio Haxford?"

It's a good job Cappy the Cat didn't paw me for food right then. I was so stunned he would have knocked me over.

"I…" I was struck dumb but I didn't need to say so.

"You'll have to be more fluent than that on the wireless, chickadee, ha-ha-ha. I'm on air right now, and Manfred Mann is about to finish. Can you pop in sometime around lunchtime and I'll talk to you about the idea?"

"Yes. Yes, of course."

"You know where we are. Top gallery of the market hall. Just when you're ready, Christine."

And with that he ended the call.

I don't know how long I stood there, staring at my reflection in the wardrobe mirror. To me it looked like Christine Capper, vlogger, blogger private eye, but if Reggie had his way with me, it would soon be Christine Capper, vlogger, blogger, private eye and broadcaster. By 'had his way with me', I don't mean… but you couldn't possibly have thought that, could you?

I would have to get a move on. I had to speak to Kim, see what she could tell me, and it was already ten o'clock.

Ten minutes later, suitably dolled up, plenty of slap and lip gloss in place (anything to impress Reggie) I stepped out into the rainy morning and climbed into my trusty, not so rusty Renault for the brief journey into town.

Duplicity goes hand in hand with private investigation, particularly when surreptitiously interrogating a suspect. You pretended to be a friend which disguised your secretive grilling of them and masked the pumping for information as chit-chat, gossip.

In this case, however, I had committed a cardinal sin. I had lied to Eileen. The client. Shock! Horror! My reason for calling at the public library had nothing to do with checking the electoral roll. That was listed by address not alphabetically. I wanted to speak to my old friend, Kim Aspinall.

About seven or eight years younger than me, I'd known Kim for most of her forty-something years. It stemmed from my mother's friendship with Kim's mother. An enthusiastic brunette (Kim, not her mother) she had been a fixture at Haxford Public Library for over ten years and was now settled in a relationship with Alden Upley, a pedantic pain in the posterior who managed the library. Kim took pity on him when his wife was murdered by the Graveyard Poisoner. She put him up at her place for a short time and it didn't take long for him to move from her spare room to her bed, and there was talk of marriage in the near future. As an idea, it had more to do with Alden than Kim. She'd been in more than one relationship and had never been troubled by the thought of nuptials.

And her past was the reason I needed to speak to her.

Eileen had been at pains to stress the innocence of her lover, Wayne Pearson. She could be right, she could be wrong, but that name struck a chord with me.

Up to about twelve months prior to teaming up with Alden, Kim had been in a stable-ish relationship for about three years with a man named Wayne Peason, although that's not what Kim called him after he upped sticks and walked out on her. Peason, Pearson? I'm often at pains to stress that Haxford is a small town, and that being the case, what were the chances of finding two men with similar names, moreover, two men with a penchant for jumping into bed with any willing female? Kim would know.

Eileen insisted that she had no photographs of her former lover, or at best, she might have an old one kicking around the house. I had only met Wayne Peason a few times, so I had only slight knowledge to go on. He was about the right age, possibly just turned forty now, and a good five or more years younger than Kim. But I never got to know much about him. Tall, good looking, with a glib tongue, but my knowledge of him ended there, so I was depending entirely on Kim's ingrained experience of Peason to judge whether he was Pearson.

The rain had eased by the time I changed and climbed behind the wheel of my compact Renault for the drive down into Haxford, and when I parked behind the library, I was convinced I'd seen a glimmer of sunshine coming through the cloud. I was wrong. It was one of those modern streetlamps which operate on light sensors, and thanks to the gloomy skies, it couldn't make up its mind whether it was day or night.

Haxford Public Library was popular with readers and (according to Alden Upley) layabouts alike. The readers borrowed books – why else would they be in the library – the layabouts, or as Alden described them, the barflies, tended to congregate in the reading room. Most of them were getting on in years, and to a man (and woman) they were unemployed, even unemployable. To lend verisimilitude to their presence, they skimmed through the morning newspapers or took books from the shelves and pretended to read them while discussing such vital topics as the chances of scrounging a couple of free pints in the Engine House or the odds on the favourite winning the 2:30 at Kempton Park.

Alden was busy with people at the counter when I walked in. He nodded a brief greeting to me, and I moved on to Kim who was returning books to the shelves.

"Hiya, Chrissy. Funny you should be here. I had that old sow in earlier, that Eileen McCrudden, her as is looking to get elected to Parliament. She was asking for a private eye, and I gave her your address. I would have given her your number, but she insisted she had to speak to you alone and in private." Kim giggled. "Sounded like she wants someone to take in her dirty washing."

I glanced around to ensure no one was paying us particular attention. No one aside from Alden, that is, who was always interested when Kim was talking to someone other than him. "I've already spoken to her, Kim, and you're right, it is dirty washing, but she wants to try to keep it in the basket rather than hanging it out to dry. It concerns an, er, indiscretion. I won't go into detail, but she gave me a name, and I thought I'd better check with you before I go any further. Wayne Pearson."

Her eyes widened. "Pearson? Not Peason?"

"That's what she told me, but the minute she mentioned the name, I thought of your ex."

"Have you got a picture of the guy?"

"No. Only copies of some, rather juicy letters they wrote to each other."

She frowned. "Well, I might be able to tell you something from them, but no guarantees. How long ago was this?"

"Ten years. It's before you met him, isn't it?"

"Yes. But he always had a bit of a rep for putting it about, and let's face it, he left me for another bimbo, didn't he?"

"You don't happen to know where he's living?"

"Mafeking Avenue last I heard. He was bunking down in a flat there. Number seventy-nine, I think. Not that I'm interested, natch." Kim glanced at her trolley, and with just a few books to be put back on the shelves and the time coming up to 11 o'clock, she suggested, "Why don't you sit yourself in the staff room, switch the kettle on, I'll be with you in a few minutes. Get three beakers ready. One for you, one for me, one for Alden, and when I come through, we'll have a natter and you can show me these letters. I might be able to tell you if it's his handwriting."

I hesitated and then capitulated. "All right, but it's on the understanding, Kim, that it is absolutely top-secret."

She smiled. "I wouldn't say anything to anyone. I might post it on Twitter, but I won't actually say anything."

I knew her well enough to know that she could be a gossip when she chose, and she would be almost certain to tell Alden, but to his credit (and as far as I was concerned he didn't have much to offer in the way of credit) Alden did not indulge in gossip.

I became quite familiar with the staff rest room during the Graveyard Poisoner inquiry. A little larger than your average airing cupboard, it held a desk, a small table, three chairs and tea/coffee making materials. A quick nod to Alden as I passed behind the counter was greeted by one from him, granting me permission to enter their enclave, where I did as Kim asked, prepared three beakers and switched on the kettle.

And while I waited, I checked again the images Eileen had sent from her phone. Small, by which I mean smaller than they probably were on her email package, even on full screen they were difficult to read on the smartphone, but by expanding them here and there, odd phrases leapt out at me. They were enough to make my hair curl. Even if I was interested in such practices, I still couldn't bring myself to describe them in such basic terms. And these were the letters from Eileen to Wayne, whom she described as 'my darling nuddy-stud'. His replies were just as candid, the terms of reference just as base, and I found the whole sequence quite disgusting and dist rbing. No wonder she wanted them kept quiet. Quiet? They should have been buried in a wedge of concrete thick enough and tough enough to withstand a direct hit from a nuclear missile. And she was right. If this ever got out, her political career would be ashes.

They also called into question the attitude of her

husband. If he'd seen them – and she had assured me that he was aware of them even if he had not actually read them – how did he ever bring himself to forgive her? Unless he was of the same bent but had never found the wherewithal to put the proposition to his wife.

Kim was much more blasé about them. Skimming through them she chuckled in places and once over, she laughed out loud. I always felt I'd had a broadly-based and open-minded upbringing but at the side of her, I had been reared in sheltered, near Victorian ignorance.

She handed back the phone. "I wouldn't swear that it was Wayne, and it was before I met him, so he could well have been in Lancaster when Ms snooty drawers says. I know he moved about a bit before we got together."

"What would he be doing on a refresher course for teachers? I mean you never said he was a teacher."

"He wasn't. He was a dogsbody. Done all sorts of work in his time. Labouring on the buildings, worked on the bin wagons, and he even did a stint as a doorman at a club in Wakefield. When I was with him, he was selling bits and pieces over the internet. Making a butty, he was, but enough for us with my wages."

"So, I repeat, how did he get himself on a refresher course for teachers?"

Kim guzzled her tea. "Remember, Chrissy, we don't know that this was him. The guy's name really could be Pearson, but if it was my Wayne, he probably blagged his way into it. He was a smooth talker, you know." She laughed and aimed a finger at my phone. "So was he, this Wayne Pearson or whoever he was." Another gulp of tea disappeared. "Course, you didn't know my Wayne that well, did you? Chat? He could charm the knickers off a restful virgin."

"I assume you mean a vestal virgin."

"I know it was some woman who hadn't found the right man."

I let her ignorance go. I could have been there all day trying to educate her on the Temple of Vesta. "Suppose it really was your Wayne?" I asked.

She shrugged. "Dunno what difference it would make to me. It were ten years ago, you say? That makes it a good six or seven years before I met him."

"But would Wayne Peason resort to blackmail?"

"I wouldn't put it past him, especially if he's broke. And before you ask, I don't know one way or the other. The night he packed up and left, I told him exactly what I thought of him, and I warned him that if he ever came near me again, I wouldn't leave enough for the police to bring any charges, and what I did leave would be singing soprano."

Despite my well-known objection to violence, often reiterated on my vlog, it was an attitude I could understand. Not that it would ever affect me. If Dennis were going to leave me, it wouldn't be for another woman. Not unless she owned a 1947 Ford Prefect.

"Who's he with now, Kim?"

"Don't know, don't care. I know he shipped in with some saleswoman from the electrical department at CutCost. You know the kind I mean. They're always badgering you to buy a new cooker or washer or fridge and stuff, and when you do buy one, they nag you to take out an extended warranty on it. The place on Mafeking Avenue was hers, but I don't know if he's still with her."

"You don't know her name?"

"Janice Robertson, I think. She still works at CutCost. I see her now and then, but she doesn't try to sell me anything."

And I could understand why.

I finished my tea, put the cup in the sink, and said, "That's great, Kim. Thanks for bringing me up to speed, and remember, these letters are super-secret. Not a word to anyone."

"I'll keep mum."

"Especially not to your mum," I said with memories of Joan Aspinall, one of Haxford's biggest gossips, at the front of my mind.

Chapter Five

Haxford market hall was a relatively new building, put up in the mid-seventies after the original, Victorian/Edwardian hall burned down. It was never clear how the old building came to go up in smoke and flames which some commentators insisted could be seen from Huddersfield. There were many suggestions as to the cause of the fire, most of them centred around deliberate action from one or more stallholders eager to cash in on their insurance. That kind of allegation was typical of the Haxford gossip merchants, but although the fire service found evidence of deliberate firing, the police never had enough to prosecute any individual. Fingers were pointed, certainly, but nothing ever came of it, and the WDIG (Woollen District Insurance Group) paid out an awful lot of money, not only to Haxford Borough Council for the building and lost rents but also to the stallholders who lost stock and profits while waiting for the place to be rebuilt.

The new hall was a smart, well laid out place, but according to my mother it lacked the ambience and character of the original. I made no excuses for being a frequent visitor. There were plenty of bargains in shops on the High Street, but so many of them were small town branches of national chains, and their service lacked that personal, good-humoured touch which came from market traders.

Radio Haxford had its 'studio' on the upper floor of the indoor market hall. I say studio, but it was more of a large office, with a small, soundproof and windowless booth at the rear where DJs like Reggie Monk did their stint. The office was not open to the general public, and a bored security guard stood outside the door to stop riffraff like me gaining access. It took several minutes to get the message across that Reggie was expecting me, and for him to confirm it via his two-way radio. I got there at just before twelve, and Reggie was bringing his program to an end, so he couldn't confirm it, and the young admin clerk to whom the security guard spoke, didn't really have a clue what was going on. According to the snippets of conversation I picked up over the two-way radio, she was busy taking sandwich orders for the lunch break.

Eventually, however, the security man got the necessary clearance, punched in the access code, and opened the door for me.

The young woman, still carrying a piece of cardboard on which she had written the sandwich orders, showed me to a seat, assured me that Reggie would be just a few minutes, and asked if I wanted anything while she was visiting the various catering stalls in the market hall. I declined. I hadn't come there for lunch, and by the look of the people in the office, they were not my type at all. Several of them were manning telephones, presumably dealing with incoming calls, while another two or three were making outgoing calls. Advertising canvassers, I guessed. Radio Haxford received grants from the local authority, but even though it concentrated on the town and its people, the crew still needed to sell advertising. They'd contacted me on several occasions, asking if I wished to advertise my services on one programme or another. I declined. There were not many people in Haxford looking for private investigators, and my vlog got all the exposure it needed via social media.

I was not a big fan of radio, but I did tune in now and then, usually on a morning if and when I had to go out, and I needed traffic reports. Other than that, the output, a mixture of varied music and chat, didn't really interest me, but I knew the station had a solid audience numbered in the thousands, which considering our population of about 25,000, wasn't a bad showing.

I knew Reggie Monk. Everyone in Haxford knew Reggie Monk. I'd had any number of mentions on his morning show which ran from eight until noon. Not adverts as such, but usually trying to raise a weak laugh with rhetorical, mock queries like, 'is that one for your weekly vlog, Christine Capper?' I'd also seen him at live events, like the Wool Fair or the Parish Church fete when he would announce whichever act had been scraped from the bottom of the barrel to entertain (I use the word in its loosest possible sense) the visitors. However, I'd never met him. Indeed, before yesterday, I couldn't recall ever speaking to him.

He was somewhere in his early forties, a good decade younger than me, but he dressed as a hangover from the mid-seventies. I could barely recall disco and he was younger than me, so where he got the notion of bell bottoms and Neil Diamond type glitzy shirts bearing all sorts of wacko designs, I really don't know, and they didn't go with his jet black, heavily-gelled, teddy boy haircut. His trademark was his wholly false and insincere, ha-ha-ha laugh, so familiar to his listeners, and so habitual that he'd used it when speaking to me on the phone earlier.

I never realised how tall he was until he ended his show, threw the headphones off and came out of the broadcasting booth. Dennis stood five feet eleven inches, but Reggie was several inches taller by my reckoning. He dwarfed the middle aged elderly man he was speaking with (who I assumed was his director or producer or something).

Although he always claimed he came from the Leeds area, almost everyone knew different. He was a Haxforder who had worked the pubs and clubs of the general Leeds/Bradford area, which took in Dewsbury, Huddersfield, and as far south as Haxford and far north and west as Halifax. He was never shy to reveal that he was twice married, his first attempt having fallen at the booze and adultery fence, but he had never said whether it was he or his wife who had hit the bottle and/or strayed from the tight path of marital fidelity. If his missus found him as irritating as I did, maybe she had decided a bottle of mother's ruin or someone else's bed was preferable. Come to that, maybe she had bumped into Wayne Peason at some time. He and Reggie were about the same age, give or take a year or two.

Most of my information came from Dennis who did the service and repair work on Reggie's car and consequently knew a lot more about him. One thing I did glean from Dennis was that radio DJ-ing for a small audience like Radio Haxford, didn't pay much better than pen pushing for the local authority. Dennis estimated that on the basis that Reggie ran a ten year old Ford Focus. If he was earning a large salary, why didn't he own something more impressive?

To be fair to the man, if I found him easy to recognise, he was the same with me. Once he finished his chat with the director/producer/general factotum, he crossed the floor, a broad smile on his lips and shook hands. "Chrissy. Good of you to come. Can I get you some tea, coffee, or would you prefer something a little more, er, adult, ha-ha-ha?"

"Too early in the day for me, thank you, Reggie." I waved a hand around the busy office. "And it's a little crowded in here. Could we retire to, say, Terry's Tea Bar or somewhere like that?"

"Sure. No problem. An old friend, is Terry."

He was an old friend of mine, too, but according to regular announcements on the radio, everyone was an old friend of Reggie's. Credit where it's due, Terry greeted him with the same warmth as he did me, and less than five minutes later we were tucked into a corner table of Terry's open plan stall, drinking decent tea, and practising that small talk so familiar as a preamble to business meetings.

It didn't take Reggie long to swing the conversation to Radio Haxford and the proposition he had put to me over the phone.

"What we need, Chrissy, is someone to fill in a fifteen minute slot every Tuesday morning. It's a phone-in setup. Punters ring in and ask for advice on all sorts of issues. Anything from debt to marital problems, children to finding care for ageing parents, even which plants to set up in the garden and the best time of year for bedding them in."

I frowned. Maybe it was my memory playing tricks on me, but I was sure... "I thought you already had someone doing that. Lizzie Finister."

Reggie looked around, eyes furtive, ears pricked up like Cappy the Cat's, ever alert for the sound of something that should not be. He faced me, leaned in so close that I got a nostril full of his cheap aftershave combined with body odour, and he lowered his voice. "She got sacked, two days ago."

This was news. "What happened?"

"Politics. I said we get all sorts of birdbrains ringing in, and we screen all calls to make sure they're not asking anything we shouldn't hear, like what size bra do you take, where do you buy your frillies, ha-ha-ha." His laughter was quieter this time, but no less insincere. "This woman rang in and claimed she was going to ask how to get in touch with her MP. Bit difficult now that Cyril Utterridge is six feet under, ha-ha-ha. We put her through, she went on air, and asked Lizzie how she should vote in the by election. Lizzie should have cut the call there and then, said something like, 'we can't give that kind of advice out on the radio'. She didn't. She said, and I quote, 'Labour. Whatever you do, don't vote for that drunk, Frederica Thornton, that snooty so-and-so, Eileen

McCrudden, or that barmpot, Hal Jorry'. That was when it all hit the fan, ha-ha-ha."

Reggie resumed his normal seated position, much to the relief of my olfactory senses. He took a large swallow of tea, and then leaned forward again. By now, I was tempted to dig out one of my deodorant sprays, and give it a couple of squirts in the air between us.

"It's bias, Chrissy," he said, "and whatever we do, we cannot afford to demonstrate any bias. The switchboard was choc-a-bloc with calls afterwards, most of them complaining about her blatant canvassing for the Labour Party."

I understood. I was careful in my weekly vlog and my more frequent blogs to avoid any kind of controversy. Even when reporting on closed private investigations, I always changed names, other than with the express permission of the people concerned.

On receiving Reggie's lowdown, I added Lizzie Finister to the list of possible suspects for the blackmail of Eileen McCrudden. Anyone prepared to sacrifice their minimal broadcasting career to insist on electing Ambrose Davenport wouldn't stop at trivia like blackmail.

"That's shocking. And very unprofessional. And she's a reporter, isn't she? Lizzie? Doesn't she work for the Haxford Recorder?"

"Right on all counts. She should've known better. The boss turned up before the programme was finished, there was a stand up row and he sacked her on the spot. Thing is, Chrissy, it's an ill wind that blows no one any good, but it's created an opening, and it's a great opportunity for someone like you, someone who's quite comfortable in front of a camera or microphone, to get yourself a bit of free publicity, build up your reputation, and I mean your angelic reputation, not anything else. Ha-ha-ha."

I was at once excited and flattered. Excited at the prospect of enhancing my 'angelic reputation' if only on local radio, and flattered that they considered me before anyone else. Well, I assumed they had thought of me first. For all I knew, they could have approached another dozen people before deciding on me.

If, however, I was thrilled at the prospect, it was also quite daunting. "I'm sorry, Reggie, I'm not the best in the world when it comes to offering advice on marital problems, mainly because I don't have any. I wouldn't know how to go about finding childcare, mainly because when my granddaughter eventually goes to school, I'll be providing the childcare while her mother's at work, and what I know about planting plants, you could probably find online. Apart from that—"

He interrupted before I could get to tell him of my concerns. "Lizzie was exactly the same, but it's not a problem. We have enough people in the outer office to find the answers for you, and they'll flash up on a little computer screen in front of you. All you have to do is translate those answers into sensible advice. Sensible and friendly, that is. If someone asked you how to vote in the election, you tell them you can't answer. Whatever you do, don't tell them to eff off. Ha-ha-ha."

"I don't use language like that anyway." I sipped at my tea. If I drank much more this morning, I would be in urgent need of the nearest toilet more often than was good for me. "You said you needed someone who is comfortable in front of the camera or the microphone. Fair comment, I'm quite happy talking to the camera, but it's a webcam. I don't have an audience. I'm talking to myself, and when I make mistakes, I can go over it and do it again."

"Trust me, Chrissy, you'll soon settle into it. If it makes you any more comfortable, we'll set up a webcam so it'll be just like home. As for giving advice, you're a reasonably well-known commentator on the comings and goings around Haxford. In fact, if I'm not mistaken, it's the title of your blog, isn't it? Christine Capper's Comings and Goings. Give yourself a break, love. You never know what might come of it."

"How about a disaster?"

"Is that how you feel when you're working as a private eye? And you're an ex-cop, aren't you? Come on, Chrissy. You can do it."

My doubts must have got through to him at last. He sat back, churning the problem over in his mind, or whatever passed for his mind.

A minute later, he came back to me. "Tell you what, can you come into the studio tomorrow morning, and we'll do a live one-to-one interview."

This was even more frightening than the prospect of a weekly advice slot. "Oh, I don't know. I'm tied up in a case at the moment and…"

I trailed off, and Reggie took full advantage of my silence. "A long time ago, when I decided I didn't want to be a bus driver, I invested a small fortune in my DJ equipment and started touting round the pubs and clubs looking for a slot. I remember that first gig like it was yesterday. I was absolutely terrified, and you've no idea the number of mistakes I made. Comfort zones, Chrissy. If you're going to get anywhere in life, you have to expand them, break out of the prison most people enclose themselves in. Tomorrow morning. Half past ten. Convenient?"

His words made absolute sense to me, and I capitulated. "If it's a complete and utter catastrophe, I'll blame you in next week's vlog. One final question, Reggie. How much does this weekly thing pay?" All right, so it was mercenary, but I had a good trainer: Dennis.

"That's what I like to hear. A good, old-fashioned, Yorkshire woman. Ha-ha-ha. It doesn't pay mega dollars, Chrissy. I reckon it's about thirty quid for about an hour's work every week. You have half an hour of prep, fifteen minutes live, and a fifteen minute wind down. How does that sound?"

I gave way. "I'll be with you at half past ten tomorrow morning."

Chapter Six

Mafeking Avenue consisted of large blocks of deck access flats and maisonettes in the middle of Batley Road Estate. No one could remember why the main road was named Batley Road. It wasn't as if it went anywhere near Batley. In fact, it didn't go anywhere other than turning a large and ponderous semicircle to join Sheffield Road south of the town centre but at least Sheffield Road went to Sheffield eventually. Stranger still were the names of streets running off Batley Road. Mafeking, Sebastopol, Crecy, Flanders, all locations from the days of Empire and the various wars and skirmishes we Brits had got into. I enjoyed history at school. I even got a low grade A level in it. But I couldn't recall reading about the battle of Batley.

In common with most council estates in Haxford, the area needed serious money spending on it, money which the local authority insisted they didn't have. That was typical of Haxford Borough Council. If you asked them to spend ten pounds on sweeping the children's playground in the Barncroft Memorial Park, they'd still cry 'skint'.

The estate had a poor reputation and it wasn't the kind of place where I'd be happy to leave my car for too long, but as it happened, that wasn't a problem. I knocked on the door of number 89 half a dozen times before the young woman from next door came out and complained that I was keeping her baby awake and that Janice Robertson lived at number 79 and anyway she was probably at work. I thanked her, moved along the block, repeated the door-knock at the correct address, got no answer and hurried back to my car before anyone had the opportunity to steal the wheels. I drove out of the estate onto Batley Road for the battle across town to CutCost, which was on Huddersfield Road.

Officially it was a supermarket, but it was one of those giant, all-singing, all-dancing, we-sell-everything places, and the upper floor, as well as housing the cafeteria, was given over to clothing, music and video, mobile phones and electrical goods, by which I mean anything and everything electrical from MP3 players to TV sets, tablets to laptops, kettles and microwave ovens to cookers and fridges, vacuum cleaners to washing machines. If you had to plug it in or it ran on batteries, they sold it.

Wandering into the department, eyeing up the tall fridge freezers (I had been saying for some time that our under-the-counter-models were due for replacement) I asked a young man to point Janice Robertson out to me, and he did, but she was seated at a little desk, busy with a customer. Probably trying to sell him an extended warranty on his rechargeable flashlight.

"Can I help at all?"

"No. I really need to speak to Janice."

And so I waited.

And while I waited I wandered around the department eyeing up the various bits and pieces we could use, if I could persuade Dennis. A new cooker would be a start. Not that there was anything wrong with the one we had, but it was getting on a bit, and the number of times Dennis had managed to burn something on the hob hadn't helped maintain its pristine, white finish. If we changed the colour scheme and bought something black, it wouldn't show the scorch marks, although the wallpaper might still make a statement to his lack of culinary expertise. But then, if we bought a black cooker, I'd certainly need the black fridge/freezer to go with it, and a black washing machine and tumble dryer, neither of which appeared to be on offer. The closest they came was silver-grey.

I was debating whether they would match the black cooker, fridge, etc. when Janice came across to me, having wrapped up her business with her customer. "My colleague says you wanted to speak to me. Did you want me in particular, only we're all well trained in the various appliances—"

I cut off her sales patter before she could get into full swing. "I'm not buying," I said with a wishful eye on the black Belling cooker before me. "I want to talk about Wayne Peason."

Her polite, well-drilled sales approach disappeared as if someone had snapped their fingers and woken her from a hypnotic trance.

She was a pretty woman, slim, trim, well turned out and many years younger than Kim, and I guessed that might have been one of the factors which persuaded the fly-by-night Wayne to shift his allegiance. Yet, I could see by the way her chin jutted out and her laser blue eyes practically impaled me, that Mr Peason was not the most popular topic with her.

"Whatever he's told you, he's lying. It was nothing to do with me." The remarkable shift in character was completed by a reversion to the standard Haxford Yorkshire accent, several rungs down the ladder of Received Pronunciation from the Queen's English.

"He hasn't told me anything. I'm looking for him so he can tell me something."

"Well, I haven't seen him in yonks."

This was not going at all the way I'd planned. "Listen, Janice – you don't mind if I call you by your Christian name, do you – I need to speak to him and the last address I have for him is yours."

Her frown deepened. "Are you from the filth?"

"No. I was a police officer, many years ago. Probably before you were born. These days I'm a private investigator. Christine Capper. I'm also a vlogger and blogger, so you might have heard of me."

The look on her face told me she didn't know me from the man/woman who collected her dustbins. Perhaps I was being unfair. Maybe she was on first name terms with the man/woman who collected her dustbins.

"I'm looking into an issue where Wayne had been implicated," I concluded.

"Well, I don't know where he is or who he's living with." She glanced over at the cafeteria. "I'm due for a break in about five minutes. Any chance you could wait for me in the café?"

It was getting towards that time of day anyway, so I agreed, and took my leave of her, made my way to the cafeteria where I ordered a scone and jam and a cup of tea, and found a table on the periphery where I could watch for her.

Her immediate actions were not encouraging. When I left, she took out her phone and when I took my seat she was still involved in what appeared to be a long and serious debate with someone. Wayne Peason? Almost certainly.

Her reaction to his name might indicate that he was not her favourite person. It might also hint that he was not averse to sailing close to the wind, but then I'd gathered that much from Kim down the years. He was what we called a ducker and diver, a description that was often applied to Dennis... unfairly, I might add. By and large, my old man was honest, although I had to admit that he'd been known to cut the occasional corner. The real ducker and diver at Haxford Fixers was Lester Grimes, known to duck work and dive into the beer at the Engine House.

It was a good ten minutes before Janice consulted with a colleague, and then came to the café where she secured herself a large, plastic sandwich and a cup of coffee and joined me. I say plastic, when what I mean is the sandwich was wrapped in plastic, but from the state of the lettuce leaves hanging out from her sub, anyone could have been forgiven for thinking they were fabricated from green polythene.

She bit off a lump of bread and salad, munched

on it, swallowed and washed it down with a slug of coffee. "I've just spoken to him on the phone, and—"

"You said you hadn't seen or spoken to him for yonks."

"That's true, but I still have his phone number, and the state of his finances, he can't afford a new phone. I told him who you were and he says he's never heard of you."

"Irrelevant, but even so, he's lying. I've met him on several occasions. I'm a good friend of Kim Aspinall, his lady love before he left her for you." I hastened on before she could swallow the next chunk of her sandwich, "But I'm not working on Kim's behalf. She was glad to see the back of him."

"I know how she feels." A third bite of sandwich disappeared. Small wonder she became a saleswoman. Anyone with a mouth as big as hers was a natural for persuading people to buy appliances they didn't realise they wanted.

"He doesn't want to talk to you."

"The trouble he's in, I'm not surprised, but if he doesn't talk to me, he'll talk to the police. Either that or you will, because you know where he's living, don't you, Janice?"

It was an old trick, one of DI Paddy Quinn's favourites: don't ask, accuse. As an interrogation technique, it was underhanded and frowned upon in our more enlightened era, but it could be quite effective, as I noticed when I said it. Janice's face told me she knew all right. All I had to do now was encourage her to give me the information.

I softened my approach. "None of this has

anything to do with you, love, so you're not in any trouble. All I need is an address for him, and I'll leave you alone. You're sure he's not still living with you?"

"He's gone. He walked out on me three or four months ago. Took every penny we had in the house. He even took the car and didn't leave me enough for my bus fare to work." She waved around the cafeteria. "I had to borrow from a colleague to buy my lunch, and when I eventually caught up with him, he'd sold the car and spent the grand he got for it. And half of that money should have been mine."

"So he left you in a bit of a mess."

"A lot of a mess. I managed to borrow enough to get myself a new set of wheels – a piece of old junk, but it gets me to work and runs me about – but I'll tell you what, between people like you, the loans, and my overdraft, I'm still picking up the pieces. And I told him on the phone just now, if I ever see him again, unless I'm identifying his body in the morgue, it'll still be too soon."

I gave her my most sympathetic tut. "Kim told me he was unreliable, but she put up with him for three years."

Now her face took on an almost begging appearance. "I promise you I didn't know about her when I met him. He told me he was single, living with his mum. It was only later when we bumped into your friend in town that I learned the truth. That should have told me what he was like. But it didn't. It took me nearly a year to find out and when he walked, I was glad. Aside from the mess he left me in, that is."

Once more, I sympathised. "I've been married to the same man for thirty years and people tell me how boring Dennis is, but I don't see that. Reliable is what I see. Don't let men like Peason put you off. Now, are you going to tell me where I can find him?"

"He'll only give you a load of flannel."

"And I'm trained to get through the flannel. Janice, it's important that I speak to him. He might even be innocent, but my information is he was involved with a woman about ten years ago, and he's now threatening to go public on their affair." I saw no point in telling her that I had no such evidence. It was a case of using anything which might loosen her tongue. "It might not even be him."

"It certainly sounds like him. Who is this woman?"

"I can't tell you that. I guarantee client confidentiality. Let's just say she's well-known and the revelation would be a severe embarrassment to her."

For the first time since she thought I might be a customer, she laughed. It was no more than a snort of derision, but at least it was accompanied by a smile. She finished off her sandwich – I'd never seen anyone get through a sub that fast – gulped down more coffee and said, "She should have known better." The smiled faded. "Mind, so should I."

"She assures me he was very persuasive."

"He is. Very. And he won't hesitate, you know. You'll have to make sure your underwear is welded into place. Is he demanding money?"

"I, er… Well, I'm not at liberty to say."

"He's short of cash again." Another snort. "When isn't he? And trust me, if she doesn't pay up, he'll blab to anyone who'll listen, and the papers pay for that kind of dirt on famous people, don't they?"

"Then you can understand why my client wants him stopped."

"He won't. Not without the cash."

Privately that was my opinion too. At least it was if Wayne Pearson did turn out to be Wayne Peason.

"Where is he, Janice?"

She looked around, looked at the ceiling, looked across the cafeteria, out to the sales area, and then at her fingers devoid of any jewellery. Finally she looked at me. "He's in a bedsit. Flat three, one-ten, Cottingley Road."

As I made a note, she went on.

"It's not where he was going when he left me, but the tart he went for chucked him out in a matter of days."

"And he came back to you with his tail between his legs?"

"Yes, and went away again after getting my foot between his legs."

Chapter Seven

There was a time when the Cottingley Road part of West Haxford was considered the 'better part of town'. Even now, it was more upmarket than most other areas, although I believed that our smart little bungalow on Bracken Close would take some beating.

It consisted of grand Victorian/Edwardian houses, most of them three storeys high, and built of redbrick, blackened with age. They were perfect for breaking down into bedsitters, perfect for university students… except that we didn't have a university. Our Simon had rented a room in one of these houses when he came back from his three years at Leeds. I was never happy about it, but he was determined not to live with us at that age. He wanted his freedom.

Number 110 was close to St Asaph's church, where the body of Evelyn Upley had been found during the Graveyard Poisoner episode. It was as nondescript as any other house on the road, but as I rang the bell for Flat 3, I prayed that it wasn't on the top floor. I'd get vertigo climbing all those steps.

At least the place had an entry call system fitted as I discovered when Wayne answered.

"Who is it?"

"Christine Capper, and before you get round to denying any knowledge of me, I'm a big friend of Kim Aspinall and we've met several times. And before you try to shut me out, if you don't let me in, I'll bell Mandy Hiscoe at the police station and they'll break the door down to get at you."

"Oh, for God's sake, Chrissy. Why can't you—"

"I'm not going to stand on the doorstep arguing with you, Wayne. It's raining. Let me in and we'll talk."

"We don't have nothing to talk about."

"That's a double negative," I told him in my best schoolmistressy tones, "and it means we do have something to talk about. And even if you haven't, I have. Now let me in."

"First floor. I'll be at the door waiting for you."

The lock buzzed and I let myself in.

The hall was dirty, dingy, in need of a good clean, a coat of paint, and fresh wallpaper to cover the yellowing, graffiti smeared anaglypta. The ground floor access was lit by a single, low-wattage bulb and even though it was daylight, I found it difficult to see what was around me. Not that there was anything other than more doors and a staircase on the left, covered by a threadbare carpet. I never visited Simon when he lived in this area. He visited us instead, but the thought that he lived in a place like this when he first joined the police made me shudder.

If the downstairs was a hovel, Wayne's room was a dump to rival the Haxford recycling site. The single bed was unmade, dirty linen strewn across the uneven mattress, the single pillow without a slip. The table beneath the filthy window was littered with unwashed beakers and dishes and an overflowing ashtray, and his waste bin, which most of us would call a mop bucket without the strainer, was full to overflowing.

He wasn't much of an improvement appearance wise, either. His mass of hair had not been combed and he looked as if he hadn't shaved in days. He wore a pair of scruffy jeans and a t-shirt which had once been white but was now an indeterminate shade of grey-ish stained with tomato sauce, brown sauce and cigarette ash.

The solitary chair was piled high with socks and underwear, and short of anywhere to sit other than alongside him on the edge of the mattress, I elected to stand, and watched him roll a cigarette with nervous, jerky movements causing me to wonder whether he was about to smoke tobacco or something less legal.

"So what does she want now? Kim? I mean, we're history."

"It's nothing to do with Kim," I replied.

He jammed a cigarette the thickness of a pipe cleaner between his lips and lit it. Half of it disappeared in a brief flare, but if he noticed, it didn't seem to trouble him. "Then what do you want, Chrissy?"

"Eileen McCrudden."

He frowned. "Who?"

After such a tiring morning, I was in no mood for prevarication. "Have you taken a look at yourself, recently, Wayne? We didn't meet often, but I always had you down as smarter than this, clean, tidy, a man who knew how to dress properly, a man who could flatter Eileen McCrudden into bed ten years ago. Now look at you. Hard pressed to get my cat to share your bed, and Cappy the Cat isn't what you'd call fussy. Now tell me about Eileen McCrudden and why you think she shouldn't stand for parliament in Haxford."

His pipe cleaner had gone out. He put another light to it, pulled in the smoke, coughed a couple of times and let it out with a hiss. "I don't know what you're talking about, Chrissy, and I don't care who's in the by election. I don't do politics. And if I seduced this chick ten years ago, she must have been using a false name, cos I've never heard of Eileen McCrudder."

"McCrudden."

"Whoever. Now is that it? Only I have to get down to the job centre. If I don't make it, they'll stop my dole."

"I'll give you a lift if I have to, but first you tell me what you were doing attending a refresher course while posing as a teacher going under the name of Wayne Pearson in Lancaster ten years ago."

He pulled on a pair of shabby sports socks, slipped his feet into trainers and zipped up the Velcro straps, then gave me the blank look again. "Not sure if I've ever been to Lancaster, and my name is Peason, not Pearson. Chrissy, I haven't the foggiest idea what you're talking about. Now, is that lift to town on or not?"

I was gobsmacked. His whole demeanour was that of a man down on his luck but telling the truth, and I had wasted an entire morning chasing to the library, Mafeking Avenue, the CutCost electrical department, and here to Cottingley Road, without a shred of evidence. It was all based on the similarity between the two names. Private investigator? Private jumper to erroneous and unfounded conclusions. That was me.

"Get a move on and I'll drop you in town."

It was the least I could do having all but barged my way into his dowdy bedsit.

A quarter of an hour later I dropped him outside the Engine House pub, and I noticed right away that he did not make for the job centre, but stepped into the bar. Curious how he was short of time and looked like he was short of money when I asked him to talk to me, but he still had enough time for a quick pint before signing on.

With him out of the car, aware that I was parked on double yellow lines, I rang Eileen. "I'm struggling here," I said. "Are you sure you don't have a photograph of Wayne Pearson?"

"I said I may have one at home. I'll send it by text or email later this afternoon if that's all right?"

"The sooner the better, Eileen. Without it I'm not gonna get much further forward."

I was about to drive away, even though I didn't know where I was going, when a familiar face walked out of the Engine House.

Lester Grimes beamed upon my car, and before I could do anything, opened the passenger door and dropped into the seat. "Hey up, Chrissy. Good of you to turn up and offer me a lift back to the mill."

"I wasn't going that way, Lester."

"Aw, go on. I'm late getting back as it is, and your Dennis'll only moan at me. And it's not much out of the way, is it?"

"How do you know? You don't know where I'm going."

He chuckled mischievously. "Oh, aye? Got another bloke on the side, have you?" He cackled. "You're letting me down, Chrissy. I always figured if you wanted someone else, you'd come to me first."

"Keep on dreaming, Lester, and while you're dreaming, shut the door and put your seatbelt on."

I had no intentions of going anywhere near Haxford Mill, but it would be churlish to refuse one of Dennis's business partners, especially since Lester no longer had a driving licence. He let it go after being banned for drunk-driving several years previously. Well, it was either that or give up the beer, and in Lester's eyes it was no contest.

While we drove along, I thought I might as well see what he knew about the forthcoming by-election. "Do you know who the candidates are?" I asked after posing the question.

"Only the one I'm voting for. Hal Jorry."

Negotiating the southern bypass, I frowned. "He's the Independent, isn't he? Home rule for Haxford or something like that."

"Summat like that, yeah. I don't really know."

"Then why are you voting for him?"

"Cos Geronimo said Jorry is the last bloke he'd vote for."

Geronimo was Tony Wharrier, Dennis's other partner in Haxford Fixers, and although there was no real needle between Lester and Tony, they rarely saw eye to eye, and whenever one of them took a stand on a particular issue, the other took the opposite point of view.

"He's a bit right wing, Lester."

"Geronimo? Right wing?"

"No. I'm talking about Jorry."

"Is he?" Lester shrugged and began to roll a cigarette. "I wouldn't know, but if Geronimo wouldn't touch him, then he's got to be the bloke for me."

"What a waste of a vote. And you can't smoke that thing in here. I'm like Dennis. I don't allow it."

"I know, I know. I'm just getting it ready for when we get back." As we turned into the mill approach, he tucked the completed cigarette in his shirt pocket. "I didn't know you were into politics, Chrissy."

"I'm not. I'm working on a case."

He laughed. "I see. Doing a bit for the MI5 now, are you?"

I slotted the car into a space between the company's van and Dennis's pride and joy, a 1979 Morris Marina. Switching off the engine, I faced him. "Mind your own business, Lester. Here you are, delivered safe and sound, now be a good little boy scout and report to my old man."

He laughed again. "That'll be the day when I have to bow to your Dennis. But remember, whenever you fancy a wild night out, you can always find me in the Sump Hole."

The Sump Hole was the local soubriquet for the Engine House.

The rain had begun to fall again. Turning up the hood of my coat, I got out of the car and hurried into the workshop where I found Dennis under the hood of a late-model Vauxhall Corsa, and Tony Wharrier stood by apparently waiting for something.

"Ah," Tony said. "The wanderer returns." He was talking about Lester, and went on, "I thought you were just nipping down to the wholesalers for spares."

"I did. They're in me pocket." Lester dipped into his pocket and pulled out a small plastic bag containing electrical connectors. "When I'm talking spares, Zorro, I don't mean great chunks of bodywork or half an engine." He pointed to his bench in the far corner, where a washing machine stood, its internal wiring exposed. "Jammy Patel will be screaming for that by tomorrow morning, so I had to go out, and as you know, I don't drive no more. If one of you'd offered to take me, I'd have been back an hour ago."

"On the basis that the Sump Hole was shut then?"

From under the hood, Dennis chimed in. "I wish you two would shut up. This front corner panel's ready for coming off, Geronimo. Get ready to catch it."

Tony moved closer, and prepared to retrieve the front panel from the vehicle, but Lester was not yet finished. "If it hadn't been for your lass, Cappy, I'd have had to wait for a bus back, as well."

At that point, Dennis emerged from under the hood, looked first at Lester, and then turned his head to look in my direction. "All right, lass. What are you doing here?"

"Providing a taxi service for your partners. I'll send you the bill."

My husband grunted. "Not me. Him." He aimed his spanner at Lester. "Give me a minute to get this panel off, and I'll make you some tea."

"No you won't. You'll take me up to Sandra's. I need a quick and quiet word with you."

"Whatever."

That was my lovely husband. Always knew when it was best not to argue.

Haxford Mill had long ago ceased to process wool. Bequeathed to Haxford Borough Council by the fabulously wealthy, now extinct, Barncroft family, it was broken down into units housing all manner of small businesses, including Haxford Fixers, who rented two large units on the ground floor. One of the focal points of the mill was Sandra's Snacky, a place where the community of employees and some of its customers could congregate over good, if simple food. It was owned and run by Sandra Limpkin, a woman I'd known for many years, and one I would describe as WYSIWYG. She called a spade a spade, tolerated no nonsense from her customers or staff, and yet she was fairly easy to get on with once you got used to her candour.

"Politics?" She was amazed when I told her I had been hired by one of the election candidates. "Parlour tricks is nearer the mark. And what does he want you to do? Dig dirt on his opponents?"

I had already said too much, so I agreed with a

thin smile and a nod.

Dennis was just as surprised when I told him of my day.

"What are you doing getting mixed up with those clowns?"

"Making fifty pounds an hour."

He gawped. "Fifty? You normally charge twenty."

"Well, the client can afford it. In the meantime, what do you know about the candidates in the election?"

Had it not been for Lester insisting on a lift back to the mill, it was a question I would never put to Dennis, because the answer was predictable. "Less than I know about the ECU on the Vauxhall Corsa I'm working on. Good God, woman, they're all crooks and liars."

"Not all of them."

"Name me one that isn't."

Determined not to shift the emphasis while I sipped at my tea, I said, "Lester said something in the car on the way here. Hal Jorry. What do you know about him?"

"He's an idiot. He's a teacher at Haxford College. Teaches mechanicking." Dennis snorted. "Mechanicking, my eye. I can outspanner him any day of the week."

"Then how come he's teaching it and you're doing it?"

"You know what they say? Them as can, do, them as can't, teach. Besides, the way you spend money, I couldn't afford the pay cut." He glugged from his cup. "He's a bigger Nazi than Hitler. Don't quote me on that, because I wouldn't know about his politics if I ran over him at a rally in Market Street, but according to Geronimo, he's in favour of re-patronising anyone who wasn't born and bred in Haxford."

"You mean repatriating."

"Do I? Happen I do. He also thinks women and children should be seen and not heard and anyone who's out of work won't be out of work for long once he's sent everyone back where they were born. According to Geronimo's calculations, by the time Jorry is finished, there'll only be about a dozen people left in Haxford, and me and you, and Geronimo and his wife, and their two lads, make up six of those twelve."

"What about our Simon and Ingrid?"

"Ingrid's living in Scarborough, and Simon married a Manchester lass, and all those who originally came from Huddersfield, Manchester, Sheffield, will be sent home, so Simon will have to go with Naomi."

Dennis guzzled his tea while I considered his description of this man. I had no doubt that Tony Wharrier was exaggerating. Dennis, on the other hand, wasn't so sure.

"If you're gonna start hassling these people, Chrissy, just be careful. I'm not saying they're out and out thugs, but a mouthpiece like Jorry won't think twice about ruining your reputation in order to shut you up."

"Which is exactly what my client is concerned about."

Chapter Eight

Longberry Trading Estate was situated on the south side of Huddersfield, about eight miles north of Haxford. It wasn't the best time of day to be driving that way, what with it being one of the busiest roads in town and the school run in progress, and it was getting on for half past three when I finally parked outside a small, neat and compact office block which boasted *McCrudden Construction (Managing Director Keith McCrudden)* and had a flashy Mercedes parked outside.

I phoned from outside Haxford Mill and after some negotiation with his PA, I spoke to McCrudden who sounded amiable enough and invited me to come along as soon as I could make it but it was on the understanding that he usually called it a day at five o'clock. I remember thinking how lucky he was. I usually carried on working until about eight in the evening, feeding the two boys in my life (Dennis and Cappy the Cat) and tidying up the detritus they left behind. Given Eileen's display of wealth, as in the large limousine parked outside my gate first thing, I imagined the McCrudden household had servants to deal with that sort of trivia. If not, it was odds on they would the moment Eileen inveigled her way into the

Westminster corridors of power.

During the half hour or so it took me to get to the place, I considered their lengthy marriage and Keith McCrudden's reaction to Eileen's affair ten years back. According to her, this man was wealthy and we all know what people with money are like, don't we? Forever bedding their secretaries in fancy hotel suites all over the world.

According to Eileen's account, he took her admission with a degree of equanimity. Did this mean he'd already done the dirty on her, or had he entertained such an idea and then decided to pay her back in kind when she confessed? If so, she never said, which probably meant the rotten so-and-so never told her and it could still be going on.

The moment I stepped into the small ante-room, I dismissed the idea. Not only were discreet hotels difficult to find in this part of the world, but his secretary looked about eighty years old and had a face (and figure) like a shrivelled prune. Yes, I know prunes are shrivelled by nature, but this was even shrivelleder... is there such a word?

McCrudden's pleasant telephone manner translated into genuine friendliness when we shook hands and he waved me to a comfortable visitor chair. He ordered tea from Miss Confidante 1937, and took the seat the other side of a coffee table.

"I must say, I was expecting a yard with all sorts of building material scattered around," I said while we waited for the tea.

"That's the other side of Huddersfield," he admitted. "This is more your administration block, where we do the books, negotiate the contracts, one thing and another. Can't haggle with developers in a shabby hut on the outskirts of Mirfield."

Eileen had said he was ten years older than her, but in fact, it looked the other way round. He was slight of build, but appeared in good health and enjoyed a glowing tan. His hair was almost gone, but I could say the same about my dad when he was in his fifties so it was no indicator.

As he talked, I also realised there were no airs and graces about him. He spoke with a local accent – why wouldn't he? – making no attempt to dress it up or make it more acceptable to his wife's potential, political colleagues, and I admired him for that. He came across as a simple working man, pretty much like Dennis, who had made good, pretty much not like Dennis who although he ran his own business had never made good, but only because he had no interest in anything other than cars.

"I were sixteen years old when I started laying bricks on the sites, lass, and by the time I were thirty, I had me own business. It's grown since then, and now… Well, I suppose Eileen's told you, I'm a millionaire a couple of times over."

"She touched on it," I admitted, even though I couldn't recall her using the word 'millionaire'. She didn't have to. That limousine was enough to get the neighbours talking.

His PA came in and set a tray of tea things on the table. "Thank you, Rowena. Hold all calls. I don't want to be disturbed while I'm with Mrs Capper."

"Very good, Mr McCrudden."

She gave me the kind of glance I would normally

associate with Dennis looking down at the mess Cappy the Cat makes when he had a touch of diarrhoea, and left us to it. I took out my notebook and pen, and after McCrudden poured tea for us, and we were settled, he led the way, once again biting the bullet.

"You're on the trail of this scroat who's threatening our lass, aren't you?" He waited for me to nod. "Aye, well, let's hope you get to him afore I do, cos if I get my hands on him…"

A coughing fit stopped him from going on and I took the opportunity to butt in.

"According to Eileen, Mr McCrudden, you have a heart condition."

"A touch of angina, that's all. Too many ciggies when I were younger. Clogged me arteries up. Don't worry, missus, I can still tackle this kind of idiot."

I didn't think so. In fact, the way his face turned bright red when he coughed, he didn't look as if he had the wherewithal to tackle my granddaughter, Bethany, and she was only three years old. I tried to remember what they taught us about first aid when I was with the police. It was getting on for thirty years ago, but at a pinch, I reckoned I could still punch his chest if he had a coronary, keep him alive until the ambulance got here, or at least until he told me what I wanted to know.

"Your wife's paying me to trace and tackle the person concerned, Mr McCrudden. We don't need you coming in with a gung-ho attitude." I pressed on before he could object. "Now, the way Eileen tells it, you were fully aware of her, er…"

If I was struggling for a polite way of putting it, he wasn't. "Jumping this kid? Aye. She told me all about it not long after it happened. I forgave her, Mrs Capper."

"Please call me Christine. I prefer informality."

"And I'm Keith. Yes, I forgave her. We had a good, strong marriage, she got drunk and fell for it. These things happen, don't they?"

I was tempted to say nothing like it had ever happened to me for all the times I might have had one or two drinks over the odds, and it wasn't necessarily because of lack of opportunity, by which of course, I mean some man spotting said opportunity and chancing his arm. I decided there was little to be gained from arguing with McCrudden.

He was still talking. "It's ten years since, isn't it? Long past. Water under t' bridge as far as I'm concerned, and I think I speak for Eileen when I say that. For it to bubble up right now is a damned nuisance."

"But a sight too opportune," I pointed out. "What I need to know from you, Keith, is anything you might be able to tell me that could pinpoint the person concerned."

"Nothing. Except, as I said to Eileen, it's probably the little scroat himself."

"But why would he pressure her into dropping out of the election rather than asking her for money?"

He drank some more tea and shrugged. A remarkable feat considering he didn't spill a drop despite his shaking hands and breathlessness.

"Hanged if I know, lass. Happen he's a raving lefty. You've no way of knowing how these peoples' minds work."

"There is another possibility. If you can think back to when you first learned of it, did you mention it to anyone at all? Even just a casual remark to a friend or confidante."

"Did I hell as like. What? Let everyone know that she'd humiliated me? Listen, Christine, there's not a lot to know about me, and most of what there is, people already know. Not everyone likes me and I don't care about that, but I'll not give 'em the opportunity to snigger behind my back. What happens in this office could become public knowledge, but what happens between me and my missus stays between me and my missus."

"Fine. That's good enough for me, Keith." I held up both hands, palms out as a gesture of surrender to his assertiveness. This man reminded me of Dennis, and if nothing else, I knew where I stood with such people. "So what about your wife's election opponents?"

He had to think a bit longer about this question, but he was just as assured when he answered. "Possible but unlikely. See, lass, I get about a bit in my day to day work, and I know a lot of people, not just from Huddersfield and Haxford, but from all over the area. Knowing them means I also get to know a bit about them. Take Ambrose Davenport, f'rinstance. The Labour man. Sound bloke, all the right policies for the workers in Haxford, but I know all about him and that little tramp he was sleeping with when his missus was delivering one of her lectures in Manchester."

I perked up on hearing this. "And does this little tramp have a name?"

"She does, but I'm not gonna tell you what it is. If anyone's gonna stitch Davvy up, it'll be me."

It was time to call on the Capper reserves of determination and pure nosiness. "He is one of my prime targets, Keith, and I'll be calling on him tomorrow. I need some kind of a lever I can use to open him up."

He thought about this for a long time, and then said, "Just mention Flossie from Failsworth. He'll know who you're on about."

I made a note of it. "Flossie from Failsworth. Failsworth as in the Manchester district?"

"The very same. More Oldham than Manchester if you want my opinion, but he's a Mancunian, is Davvy. Lawyer before he fell in love with politics. Did a lot of work with the Citizen's Advice people. Aye, and he did a lot of pleasure with Flossie. I think you'll be wasting your time, though. No way would he put pressure on Eileen to back out, not while he has skeletons in his cupboards. And besides, he's the official Labour candidate. Their dirty tricks tend to be a bit more subtle. Same goes for the Libdem woman, Frederica Thornton. Gormless sod, she is, and had a reputation for hitting the bottle once over. Supposed to have taken the cure, but it's not what you'd call public knowledge."

I continued to make rapid notes. "Someone mentioned another name this morning. Hal Jorry."

McCrudden harrumphed. "The man's a damned

idiot. Listen to him and there'll be no one left in Yorkshire, possibly no one left in the country. All he's doing is whipping up hatred against any minority he can think of, including women and children. There again, if he's found out about Eileen and her fella, I wouldn't put it past him. Only trouble is, I don't know how he can have found out. Not unless this Pearson sort is a devotee. But the fact that he's targeting Eileen shows just what a berk he is. She has an outside chance of winning, sure, but the smart money is on Davenport, and the chances of Jorry picking up Eileen's vote if she retires are slim. Most of them will go to Eileen's successor or if not, then the Libdem woman. If he really wanted to stir it, he should have gone for Davenport. One thing I will tell you about Jorry is, be careful. He won't think twice about dragging your name through the mud if you hassle him."

"I used to be a police officer, Keith. I think I can handle him." I checked my notes. "I think I have everything... oh, just one last thing. Eileen said she's not sure that she has a photograph of Pearson. She's going to check, but did you ever see images of him? Could you describe him?"

"I can do better than that, Christine." He left his seat, crossed to his desk and dug into one of the drawers from where he took a small photograph. "Eileen doesn't know I have this. It's one she took when she was seeing him. And it's all right. He's fully clothed."

"Good. Could you scan it and send it to my phone?"

He looked doubtful and glanced at the door. "I

don't want Rowena or anyone else to know about this. Can you not photograph it with your camera app?"

It was not an ideal solution, but it would have to do. He laid the picture on the desk, and I got the phone ready. As soon as I looked at the picture, my blood ran cold. Of all the lying, cheating…

Without saying anything to McCrudden, I took the picture, and made ready to leave. We spent another few minutes chatting, but I was eager to get away after my discovery.

I came out of the building at just after half past four, climbed into my car, and purposely drove away until I was out of sight of his office. Then I stopped, took out the phone and opened up the picture gallery.

The hair was tidier, the dress smarter, the face a lot younger, but if that was not Wayne Peason, I'd eat Dennis's flat cap even if it was covered in oil and grease.

Chapter Nine

I had steam coming out of my ears which turned the stop-start, irritating drive back to Haxford into a nightmare. Was it Kim or Janice or maybe both who warned me how barefaced Wayne could be, and hadn't he lived up to that legend when giving me the 'I don't know this woman and I haven't a clue what you're talking about' act?

It took me the better part of thirty-five minutes battling with traffic coming from Huddersfield or going to Huddersfield, then the hassle of getting round the Haxford town centre bypass before I pulled up outside the house on Cottingley Road where I spent the better part of another few minutes alternately ringing the bell and hammering on the door before one of his neighbours, an elderly woman with a look of thunder on her face to match mine, came out and told me Wayne had left earlier in the day with some woman in a car which looked like mine.

"Come to think of it the woman looked like you, an' all."

"It was me," I told her.

"Well, he hasn't been back, luv." She looked me up and down. "And a woman like you...? I'm surprised you're that hard up. Trust me, you can do better than him."

I was tempted to give her a piece of my mind, but it dawned on me that my earlier visit and my current agitated state were not doing my reputation any favours, and anyway, nothing I could say would change her derogatory opinion of me. So I resisted the urged, left her with a 'thanks for nothing' grunt, and marched back to my car, from where I rang Kim.

I found her less sympathetic than Wayne's neighbour. "I told you not to trust him, Chrissy."

"You did, but right now I need to put that right and I don't know where to look for him. Can you give me a hint?"

"Yes. Any and every bar, night club, and lowlife dive between here and Leeds."

"Kim—"

"No, I mean it, Chrissy. He could be anywhere, and if he's on the make, you might not see him for days. Best thing you can do is go home and take it out on Dennis and that moody cat of yours."

I cut the call, started the engine and began the slow, rush hour drive home, my anger bubbling away just below the surface, and it would not take much to trigger the explosion, as the driver of a white van discovered when he blocked me at a junction where he was determined to get out even though he did not have right of way. I gave him the standard screaming fit, and he gestured and mouthed something back at me, but because his windows were closed against the incessant rain, I couldn't hear him. Not that I needed to. His gestures were enough and even though I'm no lip-reader he used so many 'effs' in his reply that it was easy to decode.

I was as annoyed with myself as with Wayne. Kim warned me, Janice Robertson underscored that warning, and the man's devious personality was at the back of my mind when I first made the connection between Pearson and Peason. I knew, absolutely *knew* when I heard the name Pearson that it was him, and yet I let him trick me. They say there's no fool like an old fool and right then, I felt like a fool of nonagenarian magnitude.

It was a quarter to six when I walked into the house, and I was in no mood for Cappy the Cat's usual 'where have you been, I'm starving to death' routine. I encouraged him out through the conservatory door with a foot to his backside, threw a dish of food down for him and topped up his water, then finally made myself a much-needed cup of tea.

I was still fuming and it was getting worse. Dennis would be home in an hour and like Cappy the Cat, he would need feeding, and while we ate, he would regale me with his day's aggravation from timing chains, ECUs, lift pumps, and other, incomprehensible automotive bits and pieces, and if I tried to assuage my anger via talking to him, I would be wasting my breath. An introductory query on the lines of 'do you know what that Wayne Peason did to me today?' would result in a response such as, 'nothing at the side of the hassle I got from that Citroen owner'. For Dennis, nothing in the world existed other than vehicles and drivers, and the thought of the evening to come sent my temper up another couple of notches.

I made a determined effort to calm down, and rang Eileen McCrudden.

"Good evening, Christine. Do you have anything to tell me?"

"Plenty," I replied. "First, I've identified your Wayne Pearson. It's not his real name and it never was. His real name is Wayne Peason, and he was never a teacher. I spoke to him this morning and he denied any knowledge of you, and when I learned it was him, I went back, but he's disappeared."

"Oh dear. Are you absolutely sure of your facts?"

"Cast iron guaranteed. I got hold of a photograph of Wayne Pearson—"

"The one my husband keeps in his drawer at work? The one he thinks I don't know he has."

Right away I wondered just how many secrets this couple kept from one another. Dennis and I had little bits which we kept quiet… well, I did and I'm sure Dennis did too. The cost of makeup, for instance, which he was convinced came in at a couple of pounds rather than ten or fifteen. And I didn't know how much he spent on polish for his darling Morris Marina, but I was sure it was more than he spent on me last Christmas. Yet, at the side of the McCruddens we were transparent.

"That's the one," I replied. "I recognised him right away."

"You knew him?" Her level of amazement was acceptable albeit probably faked, and it begged the question did she come after me knowing that I knew him? I dismissed the idea right away. Kim had confirmed that she gave Eileen my name as well as my address.

"Until about a year and a half ago, he was living with a close friend. The same friend who put you in touch with me. Kim Aspinall."

"Ah."

That announcement went down like a lead balloon, and once more it occurred to me that she might have known Kim had been involved with Wayne. She was a politician, for God's sake. Not only was she skilled at avoiding the truth but she must have some kind of a research team working for her.

Again, I put the thought to one side. "I'll be on the lookout for him tomorrow, Eileen. The only thing I can't understand is why he isn't demanding money rather than insisting you withdraw from the election."

"Perhaps he doesn't need the money. Perhaps he's just opposed to my party's policies."

More pie in the sky. And this woman wanted to be an MP? Judging from the state of his bedsit (never mind the bedsit, look at the state of him) and the way he had taken every last penny from Janice Robertson when he walked out on her, I would say he was in dire need of money, which only added to the mystery.

I didn't tell Eileen that. Instead, I said, "Whatever his reasons, he's the one we need to get to."

"I'm very disappointed in him."

Not for the first time since I met her I had to wonder whether Eileen McCrudden lived in the real world. Given my prior, thin knowledge of him, and the accounts of Kim and Janice the saleswoman with the cavernous mouth, I didn't believe the Wayne Peason I met earlier in the day would give much of a hoot about Eileen's disappointment. I also didn't believe she would thank me for telling her so.

"I have to admit, I don't think we'll get far with him, but leave it to me and I will try my best."

I was still in a bad mood when Dennis got home an hour later, and it didn't take long for it to infect him. He was not remotely interested when I told him of my potential new career in local radio.

"Thirty quid a week? Will we put a bid in for Barncroft Mansion?"

"It's for one hour's work, Dennis."

"I make more than that in any hour of the week."

"Yes, and you spend all of it on that Morris flaming Marina, don't you?"

"No more than you spend on lipstick and warpaint."

Describing make-up, eyeshadow, eyeliner, as warpaint, served to send matters downhill, and it didn't help when I demanded his attention later in the night.

"I expect you to do your duty by me."

"That's what Nelson said to his crew at Waterloo," he retorted. "England expects every man to do his duty. The next thing he knew, someone shot him."

"Trafalgar," I corrected him.

"And the same to you."

In truth, I only suggested it to irritate him, and it

didn't happen. By the time we called it a night, he was in too bad a mood and mine hadn't lifted much, meaning neither of us was disposed to canoodling.

I lay awake for a long time, staring into the darkness and thinking about Eileen McCrudden and Wayne Peason.

An affair with an older woman was in keeping with his carefree approach to life. Any port in any hotel bedroom, although I would have expected him to target someone more attractive. Even so, there were aspects which didn't quite fit.

Writing lewd letters was one. The way he looked and behaved earlier, I had doubts that he could actually write anything more than his name when signing for his unemployment benefit, but that aside, I couldn't recall Kim ever telling me that he was the kind to write such things, and she certainly did not say anything when I showed them to her. On the other hand, would she open up about such practices? Like the rest of us, she kept her bedtime fun and games private, and the only thing I knew for sure was that when Alden had problems in that department (before his wife's untimely demise) Kim had given him the web address of several hard core adult sites. I only learned that by chance during the Graveyard Poisoner investigation, and Kim was at pains to stress that Wayne had given her the links.

So writing letters didn't fit with my impression of Wayne Peason, but blackmail did, especially after the things I learned from Kim and Janice. So why would he wait ten years to turn the screw?

Working once again on the information both

Kim and Janice gave me, I got an image of a drifter. One of those men who wandered through life making just enough to keep the dogs off his back, and the only thing that mattered was drink and dunking his digit, and he wasn't too choosy where he dunked it. He can't have been if he was bedding a woman like Eileen McCrudden.

He was obviously an opportunist, but Eileen was a common or garden teacher back then. There would have been little profit in trying to blackmail her after their brief affair. Couples talked in bed, so had Eileen discussed her future ambitions, and had he decided to hang onto the letters against the day that her grand, political designs came to fruition?

It made a sort of sense, but it brought me back to my initial stumbling block. Wayne Peason would surely be more interested in money than insisting she withdraw from the election.

The answer occurred right out of the blue, and it served only to annoy me further for the simple reason that I had not thought of it earlier. He had been bought by one of her election opponents.

As I pieced together the scenario, there was only one stumbling block. How had the buyer, let's call him that, learned of Eileen's affair with Wayne? Beyond that, it was simplicity in itself. The buyer approached Wayne, offered him X thousand pounds in order to put pressure on Eileen to withdraw, but he had to do it anonymously. The very words 'thousand pounds' preceded by a suitably large number, would be enough to get the green light shining in Wayne's mind's eye, and would he give a damn about Eileen and her ambitions? I had it on the best of authority (Kim and Janice) that Wayne Peason did not give tuppence for anyone and anything but Wayne Peason, and he told me himself that he was not interested in politics. He would snatch the buyer's arm off. And didn't Kim tell me he was IT familiar? He'd been selling bits and pieces on the internet while she was with him and he gave her the web addresses of those naughty films for Alden's benefit. Masking his true identity would be child's play.

That was it. That was how it had happened. All I had to do now was to find Wayne, pressure him into telling me who, and then confront that individual.

And with that, I drifted off into a not-quite peaceful night's sleep.

***

Friday morning came in with dark, turbulent skies, but the rain was holding off. Had we come to an end of the deluge?

Few words passed between Dennis and me before he left for work at half past seven, and even then it was me reminding him that I would be live on Radio Haxford at half past ten. He grunted by return. He was still feeling the aftermath of the previous night's arguments. The same could be said of Cappy the Cat, who regarded me with more disdain than usual, and when he came back in after his morning patrol of the garden, he didn't even give me a rub against my leg as a thank you for putting his dish down. He was a moody little moggie at the best of times, but this was exceptional and I judged it as a reflection of my anger yesterday.

I had more to concern me than my husband and cat. My mood had settled to just above the niggle mark but my focus had returned, and it was Wayne Peason in the crosshairs. AWOL yesterday, he would be home this morning, and I would be out the moment the rush-hour ended, and knocking him out of bed.

I also had my interview with Reggie Monk to consider, and like it or not, CutCost was also on the schedule. On any other week, it would be done on Thursday, but I was too busy yesterday flying from A to B to C and back to A, all of it amounting to little over nothing.

This situation was not entirely new to me. It had happened on any number of investigations in the past, particularly where they concerned infidelity. The culprits would go to many lengths to hide their guilty secrets, and that meant an awful lot of running round in ever decreasing circles for me. However, unlike a certain legendary bird, the central point of those diminishing circles would lead not to me disappearing up my own ego, but to the final exposure of love rats, male and female.

Prior experience, did not make it any easier to contend with, and Wayne Peason would suffer the cutting edge of my tongue when we came face-to-face.

Eileen McCrudden would also pay for it. According to my rough calculations (in my favour, naturally) I spent the better part of eight hours trailing around Haxford, halfway to Huddersfield, and back to Haxford on her behalf. At fifty pounds an hour, she already owed me £400, plus expenses, and with the price of petrol in a neck and neck race with the price of gas, I could add another ten or fifteen pounds in legitimate expenses to that bill.

It would not cost her much more than that. I'd worked all the answers out during the night, and I confidently expected to wrap the case up by early afternoon.

It never ceases to amaze me just how quickly plans can go astray. To settle my stomach, I chewed my way through a bowl of muesli and drank a second cup of tea, and by nine o'clock I was dressing for the day ahead. I wasn't sure whether or not it would rain again, but I knew it would be uncomfortably warm in that radio studio, so I chose a pair of denim jeans and a warm, cotton sweater, over which I would wear my trench coat, and I was debating whether to put on my court shoes or trainers when my phone rang.

It was Kim, and when I answered she sounded agitated. "Whatever is the matter?"

"It's Wayne," she wailed. "He's dead."

Chapter Ten

I was in the hall, ready for leaving the house and Kim's announcement almost floored me. I half staggered back into the front room, and perched on the settee.

"Dead?" If my voice sounded like I didn't believe it, it was because I didn't believe it. "What happened?"

"The police came knocking on my door at half past two this morning. They found Wayne's body on Greenmount Lane. They say he was run over. They're treating it as a hit and run."

I knew Greenmount Lane. Alden Upley lived there until his wife was murdered. It was one of those long roads which led off Huddersfield Road south of Barncroft Memorial Park, and wound its way for over half a mile until it joined Cottingley Road, where Wayne lived. The scenario drew itself in my mind. Wherever Wayne had been, he came back to Haxford in the early hours of the morning, probably broke, and was walking home when someone ran him down.

Kim was still talking. "They don't think there's anything suspicious about it. Probably a drunk driver who didn't bother stopping, but they're trying to build a picture of his last movements."

I knew right away that the police were wrong. It was suspicious, and it had to be linked to my inquiries of the previous day. He was at the nub of the blackmail attempt on Eileen. I reasoned sometime during the night that he had been paid for his information, or at the very least promised a payoff once Eileen retired from the election. I put myself about, asking questions, and with typical Haxford thoroughness, word had spread, possibly from Kim (inadvertent) Janice (perhaps deliberate) and Keith McCrudden's PA (compelled). I eliminated the man himself for obvious reasons. He wanted Wayne stopped, but he wasn't stupid. I knew nothing about his prune-faced secretary. For all I knew, she might be enamoured of her boss, and if she had been listening in while we were talking, via the intercom or something, maybe she had got so mad that she decided to take action on Keith's behalf.

It was nonsense of course. Until I spoke to Eileen the previous night, neither she, Keith, nor Rowena the rodent ravaging receptionist knew Wayne's true identity. The McCrudden entourage were innocent.

I soothed Kim as best I could, but it didn't help when I told her I had to ring the police. "I have no choice. They might think it's an innocent hit-and-run, but you and I know different." Even as I said it, I wondered how a hit-and-run could be described as 'innocent'. "I'll speak to Eileen McCrudden first, and then I'll have a word with Mandy Hiscoe."

"You're opening a can of worms, Chrissy."

"And as I said, Kim, I have no option."

I cut the call and spent a moment deep in thought. I was due at Radio Haxford by half past ten, but I needed to speak to both Eileen and as I had said to Kim, the police. It would be tight.

First I rang Radio Haxford and they took a message to the effect that I was with the police and I might not make it. They assured me it was fine and not to worry. They would move the slot to half an hour or an hour later for me. Another one who learned the art of speaking without listening. Move the slot? I really needed it re-scheduling for Monday, but the woman to whom I spoke told me it would be today and everything was cool. I wondered about that cardboard list she was writing out yesterday, and I made a mental note to the effect that if the proposed weekly session came to fruition, I would take a flask of tea with me. I didn't want to risk asking for coffee and her coming back with a vodka martini, stirred not shaken.

Next, I rang Eileen. Taking a leaf from her husband's book, I told her what had happened. She paid lip service to shock and sympathy, but as she went on, it was obvious that her main emotion was relief.

"I imagine this is the end of the business, then."

I took a perverse pleasure in disabusing her, and gave her an account of my overnight deductions. "If I'm right, someone got wind of my inquiries yesterday, and whoever is behind it decided that there was too big a risk of Wayne opening his mouth. No, Eileen, it's far from over. To be safe, to ensure your safety, we have to assume that someone, somewhere has hold of these letters, and is ready to use them. Now, it's your decision, but do you want me to go on?"

"If you feel you must. But I wouldn't like the police dragged into this."

Good old Eileen. A fantastic politician who would carry on living in cloud cuckoo land leaving reality to the rest of us. I repeated what I had said to Kim. "I have no choice. Wayne's death is murder, or at the very least, manslaughter. I have contacts in the police, and I will make the best effort to keep your name out of it, but I have no choice but to report it."

"I don't know that I'm happy about that, Christine."

"In that case, would you like me to prepare a final bill, and leave the matter to your good self? I'll still have to report it."

This was followed by a long silence and I could imagine her sat on the other end of the call, tossing and turning the possibilities about her head. When she finally spoke, she did not give me a direct answer. She was a politician. Why would I expect one?

"I'm doomed, aren't I? From a political point of view, that is. It's almost inevitable that this business will become public knowledge."

That was my opinion, too, and I wasn't altogether sure I wanted to carry on working on her behalf. In the twenty-four hours since we first met, she had done nothing to improve my cynical opinion of politicians.

"That's a matter for you and your conscience," I said. "If you can stand the embarrassment, then there's no reason why it should stop you seeking election to Parliament. As for the matter becoming public knowledge, well, I don't know. If I can get to the perpetrator before the police, I might be able to effect some damage limitation, but as I said yesterday, I can't guarantee it. Regardless, my duty, both as a private investigator, an ex-police officer, and an honest citizen is to report my findings to the police."

"In doing so, you will make me a suspect."

Unlikely as it seemed, it was not like the idea hadn't already occurred to me. "Can you account for your whereabouts in the early hours of this morning?"

"Of course I can. I was here, at home, in bed with my husband I might add."

"In that case, I don't think you have anything to worry about."

It was not strictly true. Once I spoke to Mandy Hiscoe, the most senior detective in Haxford CID, she would be obliged to inform her boss, DI Paddy Quinn, and he would find any number of ways of wriggling around such an alibi.

Eileen authorised me to continue investigating, and we ended the call. I took off my trench coat, returned to the kitchen, and made myself a fresh cup of tea while I rehearsed my arguments with Mandy.

She was many years younger than me, but we had been friends for a long time, and because Haxford didn't rate a detective inspector on permanent station, she answered to Quinn, who was stationed in Huddersfield. She was also a different proposition to Paddy. He operated on the principle that everyone was lying, and rather than investigate, he would accuse. Mandy was more tolerant. She was also many months pregnant and due to go on maternity leave in the next month or two. Even so, the moment I reported the matter, she would have to report to Quinn and he would come in like the SAS on rave drugs.

Settled with tea, conservatory door open on the offchance that Cappy the Cat wanted to go out (unlikely given the inclement weather) I rang her direct number.

"Chrissy. Good to hear from you, but I'm up to my neck in it."

"Hit-and-run? Wayne Peason?"

She tutted. "Talk about speed of communication, no super-computer in the world can keep pace with the Haxford gossip merchants. How in the name of handcuffs and arrest warrants did you know?"

"Apparently uniforms knocked Kim Aspinall up in the early hours of the morning. They probably assumed that she and Peason were still living together. Kim rang me twenty minutes ago. I'm guessing you're thinking drunk driver, but I have information which might put a different light on it."

"Go on." Cautious, suspicious, expecting the worst.

I gave her a brief overview of the previous day. She pressed for names, I refused to give them over the phone and asked that we could talk in private either here or at the station.

"I'll be out and about in the next quarter of an hour, so I'll call on you first. Okay?" she asked.

"I'll have the kettle on."

With at least half an hour to kill, I washed up the few dishes (there weren't enough to put in the dishwasher) spent a little time tidying the kitchen in general, and then concentrated on the living room. I wasn't particularly houseproud, but I didn't want Mandy turning up to find magazines scattered about the furniture, crumbs of food which Cappy the Cat had missed on the carpet, or my trench coat strewn across the settee. I shifted the coat, tidied the magazines, and then took the Dyson out. All right, so I was houseproud, but only when visitors were due.

I carried out a final tour of inspection, ensuring there were no incriminating knickers or underpants lying around, hid the laundry basket in the spare room and made sure the door was shut, then trailed back to the kitchen, where I switched on the kettle and prepared a couple of beakers.

As it came to the boil, the doorbell rang, and when I opened it, Mandy stepped in.

"Crap weather," she declared.

Getting on for six months pregnant, her bump was quite pronounced, straining her tight-fitting top, projecting beyond the open zipper of her fleece. Unmarried and determined to stay that way, pregnancy had done nothing to subvert her outgoing bubbliness. The life of a police officer, especially a detective, was stressful beyond belief, but Mandy had this remarkable ability to switch off, not let the job get to her. She radiated health, mother-to-be joy, and contrary to the earlier doubts about her impending motherhood, she was actively looking forward to the birth of her child. Or let's say that was how it seemed from the way she chatted when we settled in the conservatory.

I provided tea, we talked some more about parenthood, a subject upon which I was no more an expert than the next person, but I did have two children, a son and a daughter, both of whom had caused their share of problems in their younger years – Ingrid still did, especially when she fell out with her Scarborough-based boyfriend – but who were making their adequate way in the world. She knew most of it. Simon was an acting detective constable, that stage before confirmed promotion to CID, and he came under Mandy's command.

Eventually, she brought us round the business, taking out a notebook, pencilling in the date, the time, and a heading. "All right, Chrissy, give me the bottom line."

I repeated what I told her over the phone, and she made such notes as she deemed important as we went along.

"So let me get this clear. One of the candidates in the forthcoming election hired you to find out who was blackmailing him, her. Who was it?"

I hedged. "It's really quite delicate, Mandy. I'm mindful of client confidentiality."

"Round of applause, but I'm mindful of a dead man, one we're convinced was the victim of a hit-and-run, probably by a drunk driver. You're insisting that it was deliberate, an attempt to shut him up. You know the score. I need the details, and I don't give a tuppenny toss if he or she is related to the Prime Minister. Name." In response to my continued silence, she pressed further. "I don't want to report you for obstructing the police in the course of their inquiries, Chrissy. Now come on."

"Eileen McCrudden."

She made a note, then studied what she had written so far. "You're saying that Wayne Peason was blackmailing her. What price she mowed him down?"

"She has an alibi. She was with her husband all night last night."

Mandy chuckled. "As alibis go that's about as much use as a chocolate teapot, and you know it."

"I'm aware of that, Mandy, and even if you stand by what I say, we know for a fact that Quinn won't, but I believe her. As it stands, Wayne's death might not prevent the dirty washing coming into the public domain."

"What was the source of the blackmail?"

"Again, it's a bit delicate."

"So is my temper. Come on, Chrissy."

Once again I hesitated, but this time it was nothing to do with Eileen's demands for confidentiality. It was more about minimising the danger of Mandy laughing out loud.

She pressed, and I capitulated. I her told exactly what had happened ten years ago, and how the correspondence would create so much embarrassment that Eileen would have no choice but to withdraw from the election.

If I was worried about Mandy laughing aloud at the prospect, I needn't have been. She spluttered tea down the front of her shirt when I told her, and it took her the better part of a minute to stop giggling.

"Is this the same Wayne Peason who was

shacked up with Kim Aspinall for the better part of three years? What was he doing jumping into bed with a sour faced old sow like McCrudden?"

I shrugged. "Ours is not to reason why."

"I know, but given the option of do or die, if I was faced with servicing an old bat like that, I think I'd opt for the final curtain."

"You're getting sidetracked, Mandy. Someone is bringing pressure to bear to ensure that Eileen backs out of the election. That is blackmail and that is the real crime, not Wayne Peason giving Eileen the benefit of his dubious physical attributes. And before you tell me that it was obviously Wayne blackmailing her, I don't believe that. Correction, I could believe it if he was demanding money, but not to the extent of him insisting she drops out of the election. I don't know whether you ever met him. I caught up with him yesterday morning, and to look at him, he still doesn't give much of a hoot about anything other than himself. No, if it was him, he'd be demanding cash."

"In that case, if it wasn't him, why did someone mow him down? Your theory falls apart of its own weight, Chrissy."

"Not if you consider that one of the other candidates might have paid him to threaten her."

The light dawned in her eyes. "I see what you're getting at. Someone found out about their affair, tracked Peason down, and persuaded him to set up the blackmail. In that case, we still need to work out why he's been killed."

"That, I think, might be my fault. I was out and about all over the place yesterday, trying to track him down. Whoever paid him, might be getting scared that he would talk to me."

Once more, understanding came to her. "Now I see where you're coming from. It's a bit far-fetched, Chrissy, but like you I don't believe in coincidences. He's implicated in a nasty little case of blackmail, and once you start poking around, he's dead. Have you got any further with your enquiries?"

I shook my head. "I was about to start when Kim rang me this morning. And I'm supposed to be on Radio Haxford in…" I glanced at my watch. "…two minutes."

She pursed her lips. "Radio Haxford, huh? Spending your advertising budget?"

"Actually, they've fired Lizzie Finister and they're offering me the chance to take her place, but shush. Not a word to anyone."

Mandy made a final note then put pen and notebook away. "In that case, I'll leave you to it, but regarding Wayne Peason, you know the script. If you turn up anything, anything at all, you must let us know. And be careful, Chrissy. If someone really has topped him to shut him up, they won't think twice about taking you out of the game either."

"Taking me out of the game? You're beginning to sound like Paddy Quinn."

She tutted. "You sure know how to insult a girl, don't you?"

Chapter Eleven

It was quarter to eleven when I finally walked into the Radio Haxford office, where the cardboard-listing dogsbody, whose name was Olivia (surname unknown) sat me down and asked if I wanted a cup of tea. I declined. I still had visions of a vodka and dry martini turning up.

"The schedule's a bit tight, Mrs Copper—"

"It's Capper," I interrupted to correct her. "C-A-P-P-E-R. I used to be a copper, but that was a long time ago."

"Oh. Sorry. Anyway, as I was saying, the schedule's a bit tight, especially with you being late, so we're waiting for the signal from Reggie. When he gives us the thumbs up, you will go into the studio, put the headphones on, and then wait until he's introduced you and starts asking you questions." She gave me a vacuous smile. "Interesting your name being Copper and you used to be a copper, isn't it?"

I was too hyped up for the debate, so I just nodded.

The odd thing about that office was although I could see Reggie in his little booth, I couldn't hear him. There were people at various desks who were wearing headsets, and I assumed that some of them must be listening to the output rather than dealing with incoming telephone calls.

Reggie was talking into his microphone, presumably delivering his usual garrulous commentary on whatever he was talking about, and then he pushed a few buttons, and that was a cue for Olivia to pick up a headset, and announce, "Mrs Copper's here."

There was a brief pause, she put the headset down, and escorted me to the left side of the booth, pushed the door open, and practically shoved me in.

Small? It was claustrophobic. I'm sure Cappy the Cat had more room in the basket we used when we had to take him to the vet's. Reggie put a finger to his lips and waved me to a seat opposite, and indicated that I should put on the headphones.

I felt a sudden, urgent need for the toilet. The room was already possessed of an odour which I recognised from Terry's Tea Bar where it had emanated from Reggie himself. If my stomach didn't settle quickly, it could be compounded with a more earthy smell. I made a determined effort to control my gastric grumbling as Reggie spoke softly to me through the headphones.

"When this track finishes, Chrissy, I'll introduce you, and then we'll go into the Q and A session. Just relax. Just be yourself. We're a bit tight for space, so it would be better if you try not to fart. Ha-ha-ha. Trust me, it happens when people are nervous."

Perhaps it did, but I couldn't thank him for telling me, at least not in such basic terms.

"I'll try to behave as best I can, Reggie."

A minute or so later, the music faded, and Reggie's voice came over the headphones. "There you go, that was One Direction taking us back to 2014 with Night Changes. And it's not only the nights that are changing. We have our share of changes here at Radio Haxford. Ha-ha-ha. As you know, our good friend Lizzie Finister left us a couple of days ago, and the search was on for a replacement. Luckily, Haxford isn't the biggest place in the world. Come to that, it's not the biggest place in Yorkshire. Ha-ha-ha. And it didn't take us long to find a suitable replacement for darling Lizzie, and she's with me now. It's a delightful young lady, and one we all know from her weekly vlog and more frequent blogs, Christine Capper. Good morning, Christine."

There's an old theory that flattery will get you anywhere, and it certainly worked with me. Anyone who could describe me as 'delightful' and a 'young' lady got my vote. "Good morning, Reggie."

In contrast to my jittery response, Reggie's years of experience left him cool and in full control of himself and his gastric system, which is more than I could say for me.

"Great to have you on board, Christine. Everyone in Haxford knows about your weekly vlog, and you're never shy to tell us that you also work as a private investigator, which is natural because you have a history as a police officer, don't you? Can I ask why you gave up the police all those years ago?"

That was an easy question for me. It was something I'd repeated any number of times on my vlog and blog. "Family, to put no finer point on it. At the time, I was pregnant with my first child, Simon, and I wanted to be a full-time mother. My husband was earning enough to ensure that we could maintain a comfortable lifestyle, so I elected to stay at home with Simon and his sister, Ingrid, who followed a few years later."

"You must miss the police, though, or why would you choose to work as a private eye?"

I actually laughed. I didn't feel anything like calm or amused, but the thought of the stress most police officers suffered and the suggestion that I would miss it brought an unforced chuckle. "Miss it? I don't think so. In the early years, I certainly missed the, er, what's the word... camaraderie. I made a lot of friends on the force and in the community, but I was quite young at the time, and like any other young mother, I wanted to be with my children."

"That's what I like to hear. Dedicated parenting."

I had only a vague idea of Reggie's personal, marital history, but the whisper was he'd been married twice, and his first wife threw him out on the grounds of near-alcoholism and infidelity on one side or the other. As far as I knew, he had children with his first wife, but not with version 2.0.

Reggie was rabbiting on. "Your work as a commentator on life in and around Haxford, and as a private investigator, must give you great insight into all sorts of problems people come across, which, of course, is why we're asking you to fill in the Tuesday slot vacated by our good friend, Lizzie. Are you working on anything at the moment?"

"Well, my vlog has concentrated on the weather this week. It's the worst rain we've seen in many years, isn't it? From the point of view of the private investigator, yes, I'm working on a case."

"Here we go, folks. Down to the nitty-gritty, all the dirty secrets of you Haxford scallies coming out into the open. Ha-ha-ha. Can you tell us what the case is about, Christine?"

"I'm sorry, Reggie, I can't. When people approach me for private investigations, or even to feature on my vlog, I guarantee absolute confidentiality. I'm like the NHS, or your solicitor. No names, no pack drill is my motto. All I can say is, as you suggested, it's a dirty business, and nothing would persuade me to divulge even the slightest of details."

"Ooh. The Mafia are alive and well in Haxford, and confronted with the forces of law and order in the shape of super-heroine, Christine Capper. Ha-ha-ha. We'll take a short break with a little music. The phone lines are already open for those of you who have any questions for Christine, but be advised, keep them clean, suitable for mixed company, and anything you say that is unrepeatable, you can repeat to me later and in private. Ha-ha-ha. And, in keeping with our theme of advice, here are Gerry and the Pacemakers from the 1960s, reassuring you that You'll Never Walk Alone… Not while you have Radio Haxford for company. Ha-ha-ha."

The music kicked in, and Reggie took the time to encourage me.

"You're doing okay, Christine. Nice and calm,

nice and relaxed. That's what we like to hear. Trust me, you will be the absolute best at this."

"You never told me I'd be dealing with a phone-in this morning, Reggie."

"Didn't I? Sorry. Must have slipped my mind. I'll ask for more water with my tea in future. Ha-ha-ha." He went on in a more serious vein. "Are you really working on something deep and dirty?"

I nodded. "You wouldn't believe it, but honestly, Reggie, as I said, I can't tell you anything at all. It's not just client confidentiality, either. There are legal implications, and aside from breaching my client's privacy, I could be jeopardising potential legal proceedings if I said a word."

"And I thought I had an exciting life. Yours must be pretty thrilling."

"Thrilling I can live without. Most cases are not like that. In fact, most of the time I'm looking for lost dogs, or lost husbands."

"And do you find them?"

It occurred to me that these were the kind of questions I would have preferred Reggie to ask when we were live, but I paid lip service to his final query. "Always. Especially the missing husbands."

"I'll bear that in mind when I decide to go missing. Ha-ha-ha."

Gerry and the Pacemakers came to an end, and Reggie focused on the microphone yet again. "How's that for a damp and dreary Friday morning? Gerry telling us we won't be alone walking through the storm. We're live here on Radio Haxford, brought to you by Pottles Pet Supplies, the only place in Haxford where you can attend to all your dog or cat's needs, and we're with Haxford's most experienced vlogger, blogger, and private eye, Christine Capper. Christine will be taking over our Tuesday advice slot from next week, replacing our much loved, long serving agony aunt, Lizzie Finister. And we have our first caller on line one. Hello, caller, you're on Radio Haxford live with me, Reggie Monk, and our new agony aunt, Christine Capper. Who are we talking to?"

"I'm Dorothy. Let me ask you, Mrs Capper, you're not known as an agony aunt, so do you really think you are qualified to give advice on diabetic peripheral neuropathy? I mean my right leg might as well not be there half the time. I have almost no feeling in it, and the skin on my feet... Well, let's say you've never seen such a mess."

In fact, she was wrong. My father suffered from type two diabetes, and I'd seen the state of his feet many a time. Worse than that, I'd seen the state of Dennis's corns when he took off those heaving great safety boots.

"I'm not a medical expert, Dorothy, but I can always tell you who to call and how to get in touch with them. Not only that, speaking from personal experience, I could advise you to try massaging tea tree oil into your feet. It works wonders on my father's feet. As for the peripheral neuropathy, I'm sorry but that's an issue for your doctor or your GP's practice nurse."

"Have you tried getting an appointment with your doctor or the practice nurse?"

"With the best will in the world, Dorothy, we're all in that boat."

It went on like this for another ten minutes, with various callers asking about all sorts of problems, culminating in one who asked if I could recommend a good mechanic. Dennis tried hard to disguise his voice, but I recognised him immediately. I wasn't about to do a Lizzie Finister and blow my potential broadcasting career out of the water before it had begun, so I didn't identify him, but I did tell him I was not in a position to give recommendations on anything.

Time was getting on, and I gave Reggie urgent signals indicating that I had more to do than sit around the Radio Haxford studio all morning.

"Okay, folks, a final call on line three, and who are we talking to?"

A gruff, male voice came over the headphones. "I'm like your guest, Reggie. No names, no pack drill. But let me ask you, Mrs Capper, are you working as a private eye for one of the election candidates?"

I don't know whether the sense of alarm which shot through me translated to my face and transmitted itself to Reggie, but I took a deep breath, brought my feelings under immediate control. I told myself I was not in a radio studio but out there, confronting a recalcitrant witness, and I knew exactly how to deal them.

"I've already made it clear that I'm not at liberty to discuss details of the case, however, if you have something to say which you feel might be germane to any of my investigations, why don't you give me your name?"

The line went dead.

"Funny guy," Reggie said, but his face was anything but funny. "And one who didn't want to be identified. And that ends our brief session with Christine Capper, Radio Haxford's new agony aunt who joins us on Tuesday next week. Thank you for coming in, Christine."

"And thank you for having me, Reggie."

"Don't believe a word she says. I've never had her. Ha-ha-ha. What more fitting way to bring it to an end with the Carpenters from sometime in the seventies saying Goodbye to Love. Goodbye it might be, but you've gotta love that guitar riff. Ha-ha-ha." As the music started, Reggie switched to the private microphones, and called to the people outside. "Who put that last clown through?"

"Sorry, Reggie. He said he had a general question for Mrs C regarding her work as a private eye."

"Get a trace on the number if you can." Reggie concentrated on me. "Does that screw up your investigation?"

"No. In fact it was quite interesting. Did I handle it well enough?"

He grinned. "Sugar, you were perfect."

Chapter Twelve

I was glad to be out of the studio, out of the frenetic atmosphere of the office, and in search of a bite to eat. As always when in the market hall, I ended up at Terry's Tea Bar, where I indulged in my appetite for his toasted teacakes (perfection) and a cuppa (double perfection).

The morning had been so busy I hadn't had much time to consider the way forward in the case of Eileen McCrudden's blackmail, but as I chewed my way through the morsel of food, it became obvious to me. I needed to speak to her opposing candidates, and the people in her own party organisation.

Why did I include the Conservatives when I was acting for their candidate? It hadn't occurred to me before, but once I came out of the studio and began to plan the afternoon, I realised that whoever was paying Wayne (I was still working on the assumption that he had been paid to set up the attack) did not have to be an opponent in the strict sense of the word. It could just as easily be someone from her own party, someone who had deep-seated objections to her as a candidate or even to her personally. It could have been one of those people who rang during my debut phone in.

It was, I decided, more likely to be a member of the opposition, and what better place to start than with the party expected to win the ballot by a comfortable landslide. Which only begged the question, is there such a thing as an uncomfortable landslide in electoral terms?

For a Labour candidate, i.e. a man theoretically steeped in working class heritage, the name Ambrose Davenport sounded pretentious. Obviously Labour's links with the working classes had become blurred down the years, mainly because the term 'working class' had become just as blurred. A good number of my acquaintances whose jobs involved what Dennis would describe as real work, were content to vote other than Labour, and by the same token, there were those middle class folk, amongst them Alden Upley, an inveterate snob with anyone but Kim, who were staunch supporters of Labour.

Keith McCrudden had hinted that Davenport was a lawyer, a Manchester man who had earned his solidarity credits working for the CAB. Whether he had a home here in Haxford, I wasn't sure, but his election HQ was in the function room of Haxford Labour Club which I suppose was logical enough. Eileen McCrudden had set up her campaign in the Conservative Club a few streets away, while the Libdem candidate, Frederica Thornton was using one of the rooms at Haxford Social Club, yet another few streets away, the very place Dennis and I had our free-for-all wedding reception all those years ago.

It was all very handy for me. It meant I could

leave my car where it was parked behind the market hall, and walk to all three places.

I started with the Labour Club for no other reason than it was closest to the market. A low rise, redbrick building set in one of the quieter areas of the town centre, were it not for the election, I would have to be a member or sign in as a guest before I would be permitted access, but the moment I mentioned Davenport's name, the elderly doorman waved me through and into the concert room, from where I passed into the games room.

It was quiet. Four men playing snooker, a card school over in one corner, three other men throwing darts, and one woman propping up the bar, talking to the steward. I soon identified the woman as Lizzie Finister.

A bottle blonde, about forty years of age, she regarded me with eyes of ice and defiance. "Well, well, well, Chrissy Capper. Didn't take you long to jump into my old shoes, did it?"

If this woman thought I was a pushover, she had another think coming. "I didn't ask, Lizzie. I was approached, and although I didn't listen to your phone in on Tuesday, I've been told the reason why you were fired. What are you doing here? Backing up your support of Ambrose Davenport?"

Her scowl deepened. "I've been suspended from the Recorder. Political bias. Political bullpoop. Ian ruddy Noiland supporting the flaming Tories."

I tutted unsympathetically. "You're a reporter, Lizzie, so rumour has it. You should know better. You and I are not that much dissimilar, and you should have held the neutral ground. Anyway, I'm not here to talk to you. I'm here to talk to Davvy, and I'm sure you can get me an audience."

She took a healthy wet from what looked like a gin and tonic. "Not up to me, is it?"

I put on a mock face of shock. "You've never even interviewed him?"

"Course I flaming well have." She aimed a finger at the door to the quiet lounge. "He's through there... if he'll speak to you."

"If he was listening to the interview with Reggie, he'll speak to me. I'll see you later."

"Not if I see you first."

I made my way from the games room into the quiet lounge, and found it anything but quiet. An entire corner of the room had been taken over by the Labour Party machine. Trestle tables were laid out, advisers sat either side of Davenport, bending his ear this way and that, and on the table was a spread of leaflets, posters, and grid type printouts, possibly spreadsheets, which I guessed would detail canvass returns.

As I approached them, Davenport looked up, and his pleasant features turned darker.

According to my reading, he was about ten years younger than me. Tall, with a commanding physicality suggesting a muscular, athletic body beneath the pristine white shirt, the whole topped off with a head of neatly trimmed, dark hair, and soft, dark blue eyes. Well, they were soft before I got to the table.

"Mrs Capper. Hardly a surprise you turning up here."

"I take it from that that you listened to my

interview, Mr Davenport."

"I did."

"And I suppose you know absolutely nothing about the unidentified idiot who called to make accusations against me?"

"And you would be right. Nothing to do with me, or my people."

"In that case, I'm sure you won't mind sparing me a few minutes."

"Party business? You want to join? You're an armchair supporter?"

"My politics and my vote, Mr Davenport, are my affair and no one else's. But I need to talk to you, and it's been said to me that all I have to do is mention Flossie from Failsworth in order to get your attention."

His two attendants, one male, one female, exchanged astonished glances, and then looked to their leader. All credit to him, he was calm personified. "Leave us for a few minutes, will you? I need to speak to Mrs Capper."

He had them well-trained. They offered no argument, but left, and I dragged a chair from another table, sat down facing him, and went on the attack.

Correction. I was about to go on the attack, when he got there first.

"If you say those words to anyone outside this room, you'll need to consult a lawyer."

"I don't think so, Mr Davenport. In fact, by the time the police get here, it'll be you who needs to consult a lawyer. Excuse me. My bad. You are a lawyer, aren't you?"

"If you have accusations to make, madam, make them, while we're alone."

"I'm not accusing, Mr Davenport. I am, however, asking questions. The unidentified caller had it right. I am working for one of your political opponents. That's not an electoral preference, by the way. It's a bona fide contract between two people. My client has been subjected to a campaign of blackmail designed to bring about his or her withdrawal from the election. Since my engagement, a vital witness has been killed, and the police will get to you. I need to satisfy myself that you are not involved. Let me rephrase that. You need to satisfy me. Not in the same way that I'm sure you satisfied Flossie from Failsworth, but you need to persuade me that you're not involved."

He did not answer immediately. He reminded me of Eileen McCrudden. He was much better looking, of course, a much better prospect all round, but the way he took his time thinking about it, called to mind the way she had done the same thing the previous day. With her I believed it was because she was reluctant to open up about the dark secrets, but with Davenport, I felt it was a politician constructing a careful, noncommittal answer.

"You will have to take my word for it, Mrs Capper, but if I was to challenge Eileen McCrudden, it would be on her policies and politics, or her ingrained snobbery, and not based on any dirty skeletons in her knicker drawer."

"Interesting."

His eyebrows rose. "Interesting? You doubt my sincerity?"

"No. Not for one moment. It's your assumption that I'm working for Eileen McCrudden. I never mentioned her."

With any common or garden person, I would have expected a blush, but Ambrose Davenport was not a normal person. He was a politician, and we all know that they have hides like a rhinoceros.

"It was not an assumption, madam, but a logical deduction, which, as a private investigator, you should know about. Who else would be worth blackmailing? Freddie Thornton? I don't think so. Her predilection for alcohol is fairly well-known. Hal Jorry? I'm sorry, but he's a neo-Nazi idiot, and his foibles, his misogynist, homophobic, racist rants are common knowledge. I don't consider the people of Haxford to be the most perspicacious in Great Britain but the feedback we're getting on the doorstep tells us that his chances of winning this election are so remote that we can forget about him. That leaves myself and Eileen McCrudden, and since I know for a fact that you're not working for me, it leaves Eileen. Have you ever met her husband? Solid, working-class stock until he made his fortune. The same can't be said of his wife. I don't care what she's told you or any of the other voters in Haxford, but she has no sympathy with them, no common ground."

With thoughts of Wayne Peason in mind, I could argue. Privately, I had come to the same conclusion about her the previous day, and yet, when she told me about her adventures with Wayne, she had had no problem finding common ground, albeit mostly horizontal, with him.

Davenport was not through talking. "Are you a betting woman, Mrs Capper? If so, I'd urge you to check with your bookie. I am the serious, odds-on favourite to win by a landslide, and it'll be interesting to see how big a dent Eileen McCrudden can make in the Labour majority in this town to judge whether the Conservatives will allow her to stand anywhere else."

I allowed a moment of silence. "Is that it?"

"Yes. Were you expecting more?"

"I don't know. What I will say is, I've only got your word for this."

"I'm a respected lawyer—"

I interrupted. "I'm not interested in your credentials, Mr Davenport. I'm interested in the death of a young man last night, a death which must be linked to this blackmail business, a death which the police have already questioned me on, and I'm sure that they will get to you. Let me ask you, can you account for your movements at about half past one, two o'clock this morning?"

"If I have to."

"Yes, well, I wouldn't rely too much on Flossie from Failsworth, if I were you."

For the first time I managed to puncture his supercilious skin. "Will you please stop prattling about Flossie from Failsworth. I don't know who you're talking about."

"Fair enough. You might not know the woman, but there are other people who do. I'll bid you good day, Mr Davenport. I would wish you luck in the forthcoming election, but I'm not really into politics, and I consider all MPs to be... Not exactly liars, but certainly less than forthcoming with the truth."

Chapter Thirteen

I was shaking when I came out of the Labour Club but it was not fear. It was the heady intoxication of excitement. I, Christine Capper, ex police officer, vlogger, blogger, private investigator, soon to be a local radio personality, had confronted one of the country's movers and shakers... or a man who wanted to be one of the country's movers and shakers. How dare I?

Most people probably thought that police service would acclimatise a body to that level of confrontation, but that is not the case at all. The top dogs, yes. They had to deal with the Ambrose Davenports of this world on a daily basis, and they got accustomed to it as they rose through the ranks. I was never a top dog. I was a humble plod, a beat bobby, a community constable, and the nearest I came to society's upper crust during my career was standing to attention with other uniforms when the mayor paid a flying visit to the station.

And having beaten Davvy (okay, so I didn't beat him but I'm sure I got a score draw) it was time to tackle Frederica Thornton, Hal Jorry, and the backroom boys and girls of Eileen's true blue army. Politicos, shake in your boots; Christine Capper is coming for you.

The Social Club, my next port of call, was just a few streets away. I had gone barely ten yards when the phone rang. Dennis.

"Hey up, lass. How are you doing?"

At least he was talking to me. "Better than I was a couple of hours ago. What do you want?"

"We was listening to you on Radio Haxford and I was just wondering why you didn't give Haxford Fixers a plug."

"Because, husband of mine, I recognised your voice, and other than that, I didn't accept the job just to give you free advertising. That's why Lizzie Finister got fired."

"Lizzie Finister was fired?"

"I told you last night, but you didn't want to listen, did you?"

"Mood you were in, is it any wonder. Still, I thought you might have given us a quick bunk up."

"Yes, and I asked you for a quick bunk up last night, but you wouldn't."

"Charming. I've never known you sink that low."

"No. Dennis. wait…"

Too late. He'd already ended the call. On reflection, I suppose my final remark was not only crude but a bit below the belt, an apposite summary considering the subject matter. Should I call him back and apologise? No point. I knew Dennis well enough to know that when he saw my name in the menu window of his phone, he wouldn't answer. Arguments like that were best left to settle while we were apart.

I recalled something my grandma told me when I

was a little girl. "Face powder might get you a man, but it's baking powder as will keep him."

Modern gender politics would frown upon that kind of old-fashioned thinking, but there was more than an element of truth in it. Dennis couldn't cook anything beyond beans on toast, and even then it was risky because the beans needed dropping into a pan and keeping an eye on. I had excellent training in the kitchen from my mother and grandmother. One of my meat and potato pies, a stalwart of the traditional Yorkshire stodge, and by the time Dennis was fed, my moodiness and final crass comment of a few moments ago would be forgotten. With luck, I might even get some of the action I taunted him with the previous night and just now.

Thinking about it, that was unlikely. After one of my pies, Dennis would be so bloated, he'd never find the energy. Those pies constituted the perfect sleeping draught, and no, I didn't lace them with Valium. I didn't have to. Once he was fed and Cappy the Cat had dealt with the leftovers, all either of them were capable of was sleep.

I doubled back into the market hall and bought half a pound (all right, 250gms) of diced beef from Silver's Butchers, where the assistant congratulated me on my Radio Haxford interview. From there I nipped into Tanvir's minimarket, next door to the Pheasant's Rest pub, and picked up and paid for a small bag of plain flour. As with Silver's, the proprietor's son applauded my performance on the radio while he took my money. Coming out into the damp streets, I smiled to myself on a level which might just qualify as smug and sadistic. My radio performance had gone down well – Lizzie Finister being the only snark so far – and by eight o'clock tonight, Dennis Capper wouldn't know what had hit him. I would be a video and radio star, and my husband would be where he belonged; under my complete control.

It wasn't often we fell out on this level. More often than not, our disagreements were no worse than skirmishes, brief flares when one or other of us said something the other did not like. Most of the time, Dennis's outspoken thoughtlessness – opening his mouth without engaging his brain – was the root cause, but I had to accept that in this instance it was me. At our time of life, the need for carnal encounters did not trouble us unduly, and I only challenged him the previous night because I was in a bad mood generated by Wayne Peason's (RIP) barefaced and utterly believable dishonesty. True, Dennis' actions in ringing the radio station while I was on air was just as devious, but not out of character. With Reggie Monk's reference to comfort zones in mind, my final, base remark on the phone, word-playing on the phrase 'bunk up', was way off limits for me.

I called back at my car, where I dropped my purchases in the boot, and then retraced my steps once again, heading for the Liberal Club and an inevitable confrontation with Frederica Thornton. I never got there. I was passing the Market Tavern when Mandy emerged, two uniforms alongside her, escorting the would-be Honourable Lady to a waiting patrol car.

I watched them drive away, then rang Mandy.

"Busy, Chrissy."

"I know. I saw you taking Frederica Thornton from the Tavern. That's a bit strong, isn't it? I mean, all you need is a statement."

"We called to her campaign HQ at the Liberal Club and they told us she was in the Tavern drinking her lunch. When we got there, she kicked off and lamped Sonny Scott. She's now under arrest for assaulting a police officer. She'll be released later this afternoon – obviously – but I reckon the LibDems will be looking for a new candidate by tomorrow morning."

"Drunk?"

"Certainly well-oiled. Where are you up to... Oh, hey, I caught your fifteen minutes of fame on Reggie Monk's show. Cool. You'll do well in the advice slot."

"It's been well-received according to what I've been told." I saw no point in stressing that only two people had congratulated me so far. "But I haven't tracked down the idiot who rang and shouted about my client in everything but name."

"And that's it?"

"Slightly more. I went to see Davenport at the labour HQ, and he denies all knowledge of blackmail, or encouraging any of his sidekicks to ring Radio Haxford."

"He's my next target."

"Yes, well, don't mention Flossie from Failsworth or he'll throw a paddy. And talking of Paddy, has your boss rode into town yet?"

"He was in some kind of conference with the top brass when I rang this morning. Don't worry,

Chrissy. He'll get here."

I laughed. "Worry? Me? Haven't you heard? I'm the new voice of Radio Haxford... well, on a Tuesday morning anyway. I can buy and sell the Paddy Quinns of this world. Seriously, Mandy, if he starts getting out of his pram – what do I mean if? – refer him to me."

"Count on it."

With the LibDem candidate out of the game – I wouldn't need to speak to her because Mandy would tell me everything I needed to know – I was left with two final options. The Conservative Club and Eileen's entourage, and Hal Jorry at the College.

It was a difficult choice. It would be better to pick up Jorry at the end of the working day, but by the same token, I really couldn't approach Eileen's team without speaking to her first.

With rain threatening, I stepped back into the market hall, made my way to Terry's, ordered another cup of his perfect tea, and tucked myself into a corner, and rang it.

"Good morning again, Christine. I heard your performance on Radio Haxford, and I must say, you're a natural. You handled that mystery caller well, but I have to say I was somewhat disturbed at his apparent knowledge."

"You're not alone, and I am still making inquiries. Don't worry, Eileen, I'll find him."

"Good. Do you have news for me?"

I glanced around, ensuring no one was taking particular notice, and kept my voice down. "Not as such. I challenged Ambrose Davenport, but he denies any knowledge of our, er, problem." I hesitated for a moment. Would it be right to tell her that Davenport had guessed that she was the object of the investigation? I decided it wouldn't. "But I have had another thought, and it concerns your support team."

"Nonstarter."

"Hear me out, please. I don't understand the selection process for such events as this, but let's think about what's happened so far. In my opinion, Wayne has spoken to someone else, or been bought. Is it possible that one of your competitors in the selection process could be trying to destabilise your candidacy?"

The question was greeted with a lengthy silence, and for a moment, I thought I'd lost the connection. But then she spoke. "I have to confess, it was something that occurred to me when I first received the damning material, but it's highly unlikely. You said you believe in straight talking, Christine, so let me follow your example. My chances of winning the week after next are slender. There was only one other candidate appearing before the selection panel, and he was from somewhere south of Birmingham. He knew next to nothing about Haxford, and if I decide to retire from the election, he's unlikely to be appointed. The local Conservative Association want someone who will put the needs of the local constituency and community first. He was one of those men trying to get into mainstream politics on the basis that he would eventually be promoted to a ministerial position. I don't know how much you're aware of

Westminster processes, but junior ministers tend to spend as much time pandering to the needs of government as they do to their constituency."

"Fine. I accept that. But what about the people around you? Your campaign team? Are there no potential candidates amongst that number?"

"Not as far as I'm aware."

For my next question, I kept my voice not much above a whisper. "Do they know about the blackmail?"

"No, and I would prefer that they didn't."

Was it time to tell her that the police were aware of the issue? Well, if I didn't, it wouldn't take her long to find out when Mandy paid her a call. "It's inevitable that they'll learn about it, Eileen. In the light of Wayne's death, the police already know everything, and although Sergeant Hiscoe will try to keep it under wraps, she still has to question anyone and everyone in the proximity of this affair."

I could hear the disappointment in her voice. "I'll get in touch with the association, and tell them I'm standing down."

"That's your decision. I'm sorry, but I did say this morning that I'd have to speak to the police, and I tried my utmost to keep your name out of it, but Mandy isn't stupid. While we're on the subject, Ambrose Davenport also guessed that it was you. I didn't confirm it, naturally, but he made the necessary connections, and from what he told me, you were the only candidate for blackmail."

Now she was horrified. "He knows everything?"

"No. He doesn't know the substance of the blackmailer's allegations, and I repeat, I did not confirm that it was you."

"I suppose it was inevitable. He's an astute man, you know."

"I'm sorry. I have to ask you again, Eileen, do you want me to prepare a final bill and let the matter go?"

"I have much to think about, Christine, and whether or not I choose to retire from the election, I want the perpetrator brought to justice. Even if that means embarrassing myself beyond the pale. I'll make my own enquiries with the members of my team, please carry on with your enquiries."

"Fine. I'll get on with it."

Chapter Fourteen

With Eileen's decision to badger the people at the Conservative Association, I had only one line of inquiry left open; Hal Jorry. I needed an approach. Barging in, accusing him, à la Paddy Quinn, would only result in bald denials.

An idea occurred to me and I picked up my phone again, but before I could dial, Terry came from behind his counter, leaving the work to his two female assistants, brought me a fresh cup of tea, and sat with me.

"It's on the house, Chrissy."

"That's kind of you, Terry. To what do I owe the honour?" I wasn't so naïve as to believe in free lunches, especially in Haxford.

"I heard you rattling with Reggie Monk. Great stuff, Chrissy. You were born for radio."

I blushed. "Radio? Not TV?"

He put on the face of mock consideration, as if he were thinking about the proposition. "You're probably right. You're a good-looking woman for your age, so you'd probably go down well on telly."

I accepted the cack-handed compliment. It would have been better if he hadn't qualified it by using the words 'for your age' but we middle-aged beggars were hardly in a position to be picky. "So I get a free cup of tea."

"Least I can do, flower. Tell you what, though, if you're taking over the Tuesday slot from Lizzie misery guts, is there any chance of getting the odd mention during your fifteen minutes of fame?"

I gave a long sigh. "Not you as well. I've already had Dennis on asking me if I can give Haxford Fixers a couple of free plugs."

He chuckled. "Was that him trying to disguise his voice?"

"The very man. And that's not the way it works, Terry, and you know it."

I looked around and noticed that his stall was fairly full. I couldn't think of a time when it wasn't, hence the need to keep my voice down when speaking to Eileen. His was not the only eatery in the market hall, but it was (IMHO) the best.

"Why do you need to advertise? You look busy enough as it is."

He pointed at the vacant stall across the aisle. "Hakim has given it up as a bad job. What with the price of gas climbing faster than a Eurofighter, people aren't spending money."

He had me wondering what a Eurofighter was. The US dollar? Japanese yen? The good old pound sterling, a currency which did a sterling job of leaving my purse?

Terry was still going on. "He wasn't making enough out of his stall, wasn't old Hakim, and I've already asked the market manager if I can take it over, expand my area just a little bit. You wouldn't believe the rents in this place."

"It's Haxford Borough Council you're talking

about, Terry, so I'd believe it."

"An arm and a leg doesn't come anywhere near it. They want your blood too. If I take the stall on, not only do I have to fork out the rent, but I've got to buy tables, chairs, and if it gets busy, I'll have to take on another part timer. You're a businesswoman, Chrissy. You know the score."

I nodded sympathetically. I didn't know the score at all because my overheads were somewhere around nil. I prepared my vlog at home, and when I was on an investigation, the client picked up all my out-of-pocket expenses, as Eileen McCrudden would soon learn.

Thoughts of my blog slotted my mind into sales gear. "Tell you what, if you decide to go ahead, why not sponsor my vlog and blog? It's not expensive. Fifty pounds will buy you a month's worth of airtime."

He pressed his lips. "Hmm. Might be worth giving it a coat of thinking about. And over and above your fees, how much free tea will it cost me?"

I giggled. "Come on. I'm only in the market once or twice a week. Surely you can stand the teabags?" I put on my serious face again. "Straight up, Terry, quite a number of people sponsor me. Sandra Limpkin at the mill, Benny Barnes on the High Street, Sonya's Hairdressing, Pottle's the pet people. I'm not short of businesses wanting to advertise on my vlog, and you turn out such wonderful toasted teacakes, that I'm sure I could slot you in."

Terry laughed, too. "I have to hand it to you. Full

marks for salesmanship."

I fluttered my eyelashes at him. "Saleswomanship in my case."

"It must run in the family. Your Dennis is a cracking salesman, too, when he's trying to convince me to take my van to him for servicing."

I put on a face of fake shock. "You mean you don't?"

"He used to deal with my old motor, but this is brand-new. Well, six months old, and it's still under manufacturer's warranty. When that runs out, your Dennis will get the work." He got to his feet. "Leave it with me. If the market lets me have the stall, I'll give you a bell."

He left, and I had to push it all to the back of my mind, step away from my saleswomanship mode, and try to remember what I was doing before he joined me.

Terry was one of those Haxford business types who remained faithful to their suppliers, and Dennis could be included on the list. He was simply the best mechanic in the town, possibly in the entire Huddersfield/Haxford area. He wasn't the cheapest, but he guaranteed his work, and he did a top-class job. And if anyone needed a reminder of the skills, Dennis was never slow to tell them. When it came to touting his ability, selling his services (why did I cringe when that phrase sprang to mind?) he was no shrinking violet.

Thoughts of Dennis prompted my feverish memory. It had been such a busy and frenetic morning, I was literally and metaphorically all over the place, but I remembered that before Terry interrupted, I was about to ring my erstwhile.

This, I knew, would be difficult. I would have to ring a couple of times before he answered, and when I put the proposition to him, he would inevitably misunderstand, and that could prompt another argument. I would need all my reserves of patience, most of which had dissipated during the excitement of the morning.

I rang him, he cut the call off without answering. I rang again, same result. On the third attempt, he made the connection.

"What do you want, Christine? I'm busy."

There was no finer indicator of his mood than when he used my full name. At any other time I was 'Chrissy' or 'hey up, lass' but when I was Christine, it meant he had the serious hump with me.

"I want to talk to you. Why do you think I'm ringing?"

"Well it could be that you wanted to start another battle, and I don't have time."

"Dennis, you're the one starting a battle right now, and I need to speak to you. For God's sake, get last night off you. And this morning. I need to know what could be wrong with my car for me to speak to Hal Jorry."

As I anticipated, he misunderstood immediately. "If there's anything wrong with your car, I'll do it, never mind going to that waste of space."

While he ranted, I let out a mental sigh, and counted to three. "There's nothing wrong with the car, Dennis, but I need an excuse to approach him."

"What for? The bunk up I wouldn't give you last night." And with that he cut the call.

There was only so far that even Dennis could stretch my patience, and although I accepted that I was responsible earlier, this time it was all him.

I rang again, and he ignored the call.

He was leaving me in an intolerable position. I didn't want to go over to Haxford College and tackle Jorry head on. I wanted an excuse to trespass on his workshop, and the best man to lend me such an excuse was my husband. Difficult when he wasn't talking to me.

While I drank off my tea, I applied a little lateral thinking, and the solution came to me. I rang Tony Wharrier.

"Haxford Fixers, Tony Wharrier speaking."

"Tony? It's Christine."

Tony had always been more polite than Dennis or their other partner, Lester, and always addressed me by my full name. But this time he was puzzled. "Christine?"

"Yes. Christine. You know. Christine Capper. Dennis's wife."

"Oh, Lord. I'm sorry, Christine. I didn't recognise your voice. Dennis is here somewhere."

An image of the Haxford Fixers workshop came into my mind. Good friends, and colleagues they might be, but Dennis and Tony worked in different parts of the shop.

"Dennis is not speaking to me, and I need your help. Will you pop next door and tell the gormless idiot that I need to speak to him urgently, and if he doesn't answer when I ring again in five minutes, I'll come over there and shout so loud that the entire mill will hear me."

Tony chuckled. "I'll pass the message on, Christine. Give it a minute before you ring again."

I cut the call, finished my tea, thanked Terry and his crew, and made my way out of the market hall. As I emerged into the gloomy afternoon, I rang Dennis again. This time he answered right away.

He wasn't in any better mood. "For crying out loud, woman, what the bejeebers do you want?"

"Some way of approaching Hal Jorry which will put him off guard. Listen to me, Dennis. My prime suspect was killed last night. Mowed down in a hit-and-run, and it's a sight too coincidental considering the business I'm investigating. I need to speak to Jorry, but if I go barging in, he'll go on the defensive."

"I warned you yesterday to keep away from him. He's scum. And he's a crap mechanic. Take your car to him, and he'll mess it up, and like I told you, he won't think twice about blackening your name."

"There's nothing wrong with the fizzing car. I'm being paid for this gig, Dennis, so I have no choice, and I can handle the Hal Jorrys of this world as easy as I deal with you. Now tell me what could be wrong with my car that could give me an excuse for speaking to him."

He was silent for the moment, and I knew what that meant. He had finally got the message, and he was thinking of something I could use.

"Tell him the engine's missing."

The suggestion caused my annoyance to rise once again. "And how do I explain having driven it there if someone's stolen the engine?"

"I said missing, not nicked." He let out a

frustrated gasp. "How long have we been married? How many hours have I spent telling you about engines, and you still don't understand."

"That's because I'm like you, Dennis. I don't listen to your drivel. I'm on my way to the college now, and from there, I have to speak to Mandy before I go home. I'll see you when you get home. And don't be late, because I'm doing a pie."

It was amazing how quickly his mood could change, especially when his favourite food was mentioned. "A pie? A tate and meaty?"

"That's got your attention, hasn't it? I thought you deserved it after last night and this morning, but the way you've been carrying on this last ten minutes, I'm beginning to have my doubts."

"No. Don't change your mind. I'll be home for half past six."

I ended the call, satisfied with the outcome. By seven o'clock this evening, the sulky, grim atmosphere between us would be consigned to history. He would enjoy his pie, and along with Cappy the Cat he would sleep it off on the settee while repeats of Top Gear played on the TV, and I could potter on the laptop, preparing my report(s) for Eileen McCrudden, and deciding which way I would go next.

It might sound an odd situation, but by and large, I found modern TV output to be mindless dross and that was perfect for my plan. In truth, I don't know whether it was any better when we were younger, but it seemed to me that when I was in my teens and twenties, it was a golden age of TV. Mind you, my Dad said the same thing about TV in his younger years.

Whatever the outcome, peace would descend upon number 17 Bracken Close. Which was more than could be said for the automotive workshop at Haxford College.

Chapter Fifteen

The College sat on the periphery of the town centre, just off the northern bypass. A large, ungainly, glass shoebox which shouted 'office' or 'school'.

In the mid-eighties, I spent a couple of years there doing general A-levels, and scraped a couple of passes in English and History. They were enough to get me into the police service when I reached the age of eighteen. It had always been my ambition to join the police. Other girls fancied working in offices, typing, filing, making tea for their colleagues, but after X number of years cloistered in school and then college, I wanted outdoor work. Naturally, the first thing that happened when I signed on with the police was weeks and weeks of basic training in Wakefield, and when I was assigned to Haxford station, I spent the first few weeks, typing, filing, making tea for other officers, especially Constable, later Detective Inspector, Patrick Quinn. It came as a relief when I finally got out onto the beat.

As I told Reggie Monk, I gave it up when I became a mother and spent five or six years as a stay at home mum, looking after Simon and later, Ingrid. My mum took over the childcare duties while I went back out to work, doing various jobs, but again I found the enclosed, almost claustrophobic air of shops and offices, too restrictive. By the time Simon went to university and Ingrid decided she preferred Scarborough to Haxford, Dennis was making enough money to support us, and I trained as a private investigator. Under UK law, training and a licence are not a legal requirement, but I had both, and it was my proud boast that I was the only genuine, recognised private eye in the town.

Ah, such wonderful memories.

The automotive training workshops at the college were a sort of add on attached to the main college building and set off to one side. Like a large shed with walls of corrugated iron or whatever it was called these days (Dennis would know. Dennis always knew).

When I walked in, it reminded me of Haxford Fixers but on a much grander scale. There were cars on axle stands, one raised on a hydraulic lift type thing, another two stood over deep pits with trainees working under them, bits and pieces of engines and wheels on various benches about the place, and any number of apprentices faffing with them. Front and centre on the far wall was a large whiteboard, bearing incomprehensible diagrams and equally unintelligible words and calculations, as well as a list of names inked in green off to one side. I assumed these were the apprentices

Hal Jorry was talking to two young men alongside an old Vauxhall Chevette (Dennis would be drooling at the sight of it) with its hood raised.

He was clad in a white overall (Jorry, not

Dennis. White would be a waste with Dennis). Jorry was dressed rather like Terry when working behind the counter of his café, or the assistants on the butchers and delicatessen counters in the market hall. I saw another difference between Jorry and Dennis. My husband wore a navy blue boiler suit which was guaranteed to be covered in grease and oil five minutes after he got to work on Monday morning. Here we were on Friday afternoon, and despite his calling, Jorry's overall was spotless. I wondered if he had a wardrobe full of them.

There were other differences. Dennis stood five feet eleven (and a bit according to him). Jorry was at least a foot shorter. He was a good few inches shorter than my five feet four (and a bit, which bit depended on the height of the heel on my shoes at any given time) and it made a pleasant change to look down on a man instead of up. A thinning head of black hair showed too much skull and betrayed his age which I guessed to be forty-two years and three months. Okay, so I'm lying. It wasn't a guess. I looked him up before I left home. And fat? He had a gut so large that along with his bald head, he reminded me of humpty dumpty. An egg on legs.

A controversial man, he had some curious heroes: Hitler, Stalin, Robespierre; anyone who believed that freedom was intended for the elite and everyone else should just do as they were told or suffer the consequences. According to the Haxford Recorder (and Ambrose Davenport) his chances of winning the by-election were about the same as mine of winning the lottery, and it was generally accepted that he would be lucky to get his deposit back.

He was reputed to be confrontational, but standing barely five feet, I had to wonder who he had confronted to gain such a reputation. The ageing lollipop man outside St Joseph's Primary School, or the children who crossed the road in front of the lollipop man?

He noticed me, frowned and made his way across. "What can I do for you?"

"My engine," I lied. "It's missing."

He smirked. "If I was you, Christine Capper, I'd stick to yattering to your webcam instead of standing in front of me lying. If you've got a problem with your car, take it to your old man. I'm sure he'll work cheaper than me."

All those calls to Dennis and Tony Wharrier were a waste of time and however much the phone company would charge me for them, assuming they didn't fall within the scope of my free minutes.

Jorry's smug face became smugger. "And take a tip from me. Radio isn't really your bag."

That rattled me more than Lizzie Finister's attitude. "Why do you say that, Mr Jorry? Because I wouldn't comment on your idiotic question about my client?"

"Why don't you clear off before I lose my temper and do something we'll both regret?"

"Oh, I'll go, but I think you've already done something you'll regret… when the police catch up with you. For your information, Wayne Peason died when you ran him down last night."

He smiled supreme confidence. "I haven't a clue what you're talking about, but I'll tell you this.

Repeat that to anyone else, and you'll hear from my lawyers… or my associates."

So that's how he got the reputation for being confrontational. He hid behind bully boys.

I wasn't that easy to put off. "You recognised me, which tells me you must know enough about me to know that I was a police officer, and I still have a lot of friends at Haxford station. I will repeat it to them, later this afternoon."

I turned and marched out of the workshop, and as I came back out I spotted a late model Fiat 500. It was a car I'd craved ever since they first came off the production line, but Dennis wouldn't have one in the drive.

I recalled the time I first asked him. "Foreign garbage," he said running a loving hand over the bonnet of his Morris Marina. There were times when I resented that car.

I don't know what he had against the Fiat. This was a pretty little car in white with no trace of rust, unlike my trusty Clio which was getting a few years too many on its back. This example was pristine, and nearly new according to the registration. It would be perfect if it wasn't for that dent in the front bumper and the broken, nearside headlamp. Well, I say bumper, but like most cars, the Fiat didn't have a bumper, but it was in that area. I wondered when they did away with bumpers. Dennis would know. Didn't Dennis always know?

"Wanna make me an offer?"

I turned back and saw Jorry staring at me. "Interesting," I said. "It's your car and damaged right in the area you would expect if it was involved in a hit and run."

"Some idiot reversed into me."

"And your associates sorted it out, did they? Or sorted him out?"

"You're beginning to annoy me, Christine Capper."

"And you're beginning to play on my suspicious nature, Hal Jorry."

As I returned to my car, climbed behind the wheel and started the engine, he put his mobile phone to one ear (well he could hardly put it to both ears, could he) and spoke into it. As I drove away I did something I couldn't recall having done since I was a teenager pretending to be a tearaway. I gave him a two-fingered salute.

Driving out of the college grounds, I was out of options. I had nowhere else to go, no one else to speak to. And then I remembered I had to go to CutCost for the weekly shop, and Janice Robertson worked there. Did she bear a heavy enough grudge to hit her ex in the early hours of the morning? According to my estimate, yes, but my suspicions and the truth could be worlds apart.

There was only one way to find out.

Getting from the college to CutCost wasn't a difficult proposition on paper, but I was driving on roads not paper, and like any other town in the country – the world for all I knew – driving through populated areas on a Friday afternoon was a stop-start nightmare which consumed an alarming amount of petrol and patience. With the price of unleaded vying with gas to see which could climb the highest the quickest, I couldn't afford either that or the loss of patience the imaginary bill was costing me.

In order to distract my Dennis-esque, financially obsessed mind – of course I could afford it. Eileen McCrudden would be paying for most of it – I thought about the brief interlude with Jorry.

He fancied himself as a hard man. That much was obvious, and the bump to the front of his car and his mention of 'associates' was enough to persuade me that he was favourite for running down Wayne Peason in the early hours. No matter how well he had cleaned his car, there would be traces of Wayne on it.

The idea was attractive, but had a considerable stumbling block. How did he (or anyone else for that matter) know that Wayne was central to my investigation? Sure, he could have read the account of Wayne's death in the morning edition of the Recorder, or on the newspaper's website, but that only gave Wayne's name. It did not mention his potential involvement in the blackmail of a parliamentary candidate.

I was also sure that Jorry was the anonymous caller who asked about my inquiries, but again I had to ask how did he know? Someone, somewhere was talking to the wrong people, and the scenario painted itself in my mind as I sat in a queue at the traffic lights on the junction of the bypass and Huddersfield Road, waiting to turn right.

Someone tipped him off that one of his competitors was subject to attempted extortion but did not mention any names other than Wayne Peason. One or more of Jorry's associates had been detailed to track Wayne down, found him, pressured him, and when he told them where to stick their inquiries, they went after him.

However, assuming that they wanted to know the substance of Wayne's allegations and the identity of his target, killing him was counterproductive, which probably meant it was accidental. They intended hurting, not killing him.

I could see the exchange in my imagination. They made demands, Wayne, true to form, held out for a price, they threatened to rough him up or worse, he told them to try their luck (Kim had always said Wayne was capable of looking after himself) and while they dithered, he walked away. They caught up with him, he tried to run, but they hit him, realised they had gone too far, and after searching him, seeking his theoretical evidence, they drove away empty handed.

When they reported back to Jorry, he threw a fit (given his diminutive size it was more likely a spit-the-dummy-out type tantrum) and then chanced his arm by ringing Radio Haxford when I was talking to Reggie.

At that point, he had only hearsay; whispers. No convincing proof that anything was really going on in the background. He received that confirmation from an unexpected quarter; an idiot private investigator who blanked him on radio and then showed up to confront him: Christine, I'm-so-smart, Capper.

That was why he looked so cocky when I faced him. As a wannabe politician, lying was second nature to him, and he could deny it with ease, but he'd had what he wanted; confirmation that I was working for one of his election opponents. All he had to do now was find out who, and he knew exactly who to ask: Christine, I-could-be-the-next-target, Capper.

Chapter Sixteen

The car park at CutCost covered about… oh, I don't know. Let's say a couple of football fields, or maybe one and a half. Or maybe… well, it was big. Let's leave it at that. Not only big, but at this hour on a damp Friday afternoon, it was packed, and even when I found a space, I had a long walk to the store. This was not calculated to do my irritation any favours, but it turned out lucky because I bumped into Janice Robertson as I got out of the car.

"Oh, hello, Janice." I put on my commiseration face. "I heard about Wayne. I'm so sorry."

"Why? I'm not." Carrying a couple of bags of shopping, she appeared tired, drawn, near exhausted from her day's work, but her face fell further. "That sounds rotten, doesn't it?"

"Speaking as a neutral observer, yes. Speaking as a woman and one who's had the bottom line on Wayne Peason from a couple of sources, it sounds about right. Have the police been to see you?"

"Yeah. Some guy called Capper." She half smiled. "God, he was tasty. I'll tell you what, if I'd been hooked up to him, I woulda been a lot more upset when he walked."

I returned the smile. To think other women

actually fancied my boy. I'm sure he gets his good looks from me. "He's my son."

Now it was horror. "Oh, my god. I'm sorry."

I chuckled. "You would be if his wife heard you talking about him in those terms. Listen, Janice, I don't want to hold you up, but Wayne was in a lot of trouble, and the chances are he was run down deliberately."

"I know. This copper – sorry – your lad told me. He didn't say what it was all about, obviously, and like I told him, I don't know anything about what Wayne's been up to since he walked out on me. I don't wanna know, either. Now, if you'll excuse me, I want to get home."

"Of course. And thanks for your help yesterday… Oh, while I think on, if I drag my husband in here over the weekend, is there any danger you could run us through your various kitchen appliances? Only I'm thinking of renewing the lot, but I want it in black."

Her eyes lit up, probably at the thought of her commission. "Make sure you ask for me. I'll get you the best deal."

I went on my way feeling quite pleased, which was more than I would be able to say about Dennis when he found out. The announcement would have to be made at the right time; i.e. when he was full of meat and potato pie and drifting into that soporific nether world it was renowned for producing, and the follow up would have to be couched in the right terms, as in: 'You promised'. Given the right inflection, hurt, near to tears, it would make him feel guilty and the only remaining obstacle would be the price, and I'd already worked that out. I would persuade him that it was tax deductible. I did his books and by the time he came to settle his tax bill, he would have forgotten all about the new kitchen.

As I crossed the car park, I had another, pleasant surprise. Two familiar faces wrapped in CutCost hi-visibility coats, and collecting the trolleys for return to the trolley park outside the supermarket main entrance.

"If it isn't young John Frogshaw and his best pal Owen Digger Trench. What are you boys up to?"

Both aged sixteen or seventeen, they greeted me with warm, but shy and boyish smiles. I knew little about Owen, but John was the son of one of Haxford's shady, repayments-by-hook-or-crook loan sharks. The boy had cast light on the Graveyard Poisoner inquiry the previous Christmas and I found him a different proposition to his fractious, argumentative father.

"We're trolley jockeys, Mrs Capper," John told me. "We do Friday and Saturday every week. Bitta pocket money, y'know. Innat right, Digger?"

"I'm saving up for a Crater Creator Sound System," Owen told me. "Bit pricey, y'know, and Mam told me she'll go halves if I can get my half together." He was into sound effects and according to Frogshaw the younger, he wanted to break into music or movies when he was through college.

"I'm pleased to hear it, and I'd love to stop and hear about your sound system, Owen, but I have my weekly shop to do. Be good, both of you."

John winked. "If we can't be good we'll be

careful."

"And if we can't be careful, we know where to buy—"

"Yes. Thank you, Owen."

Smiling to myself at the thought of these two young men beginning to make their way in the world, wondering if they would reminisce upon it to their grandchildren fifty years from now, I carried on towards the supermarket, but I had gone less than ten yards when two men climbed out of a black BMW and blocked my way.

"Excuse me," I said and tried to go round them.

They moved to block me again, and then began to edge me towards the rear of their car. I tried to dodge again, but the fair-haired individual, sporting a rough, unkempt beard, grabbed my arm.

"Take your filthy hands off me."

"In the car," said the one on the left, a shaven headed thug about the size of a double-decker bus.

If they thought they could intimidate Christine Capper, they were... well, right as I happens, but despite my rising fear, I wasn't for backing down. "I'm sorry. My mother always taught me never to get in a car with strange men." I struggled to get away again.

The fair-haired beard turned out to be just as mean when he spoke. "We're telling, not asking."

"And suppose I shout for help?"

They both shrugged. "Whatever."

So I did. I shouted at the top of my voice, and it had the effect of first startling them, and then prompted one of them to clamp a filthy, sweaty hand over my mouth and both to grab my arms and try to bundle me into the rear of the car.

I struggled but they were far stronger than me, and the outcome was a foregone conclusion. And while I wriggled and writhed, I pressed one foot to the rim of the open door and tried to push them back.

Futile. They were far too strong for me. One of them grabbed the back of my neck, forced my head down. He applied so much pressure that I could almost feel the skin bruising.

And then I caught sight of the passenger in the rear seat. Hal Jorry.

I was doomed. They would take me somewhere quiet and secluded, and at the very least, they would beat me up. With Wayne Peason's fate at the forefront of my mind, I doubted that they would stop at a beating. My biggest fear was what they would do with me or to me before they murdered me.

The thought was too horrible to contemplate and I was determined to do all I could to prevent it. I baulked again as they tried to force me to the back seat.

"Get in the goddamned car."

"Speak English," I insisted as I struggled with them. "This is Haxford, not Fast and Furious twenty nine."

And then suddenly, the cavalry arrived.

"Get your maulers off her."

At first, I didn't recognise the voice. I was too busy thanking my lucky stars. Whoever it was, it worked. The two bruisers released me and turned to face the owner of the voice.

I cast a mean glance at Jorry and then turned to find John Frogshaw and Owen Trench squaring up to the two thugs.

I urged them to back off. "Don't get involved, John, Owen. I'll send for Mandy Hiscoe."

"It's no sweat Mrs C," Owen assured me. "Me and Froggy can deal with bananas like these, easy."

"Yes, but…"

I didn't get to say another word as shaven head rushed forward… straight into John Frogshaw's fist. The attacker staggered back, his pal came forward, only to run into a quick one-two; one kick between his legs from John and a punch to the side of the face from Owen.

"Are you leaving yet?" John asked.

With the two thugs reeling, Jorry reached across to close the door they had been trying to squeeze me through, but I took hold of it and stopped him.

Countering his attempt to pull the door shut, I dug out my phone, and with some difficulty, managed to activate the camera. Before I could take the photograph, Jorry released the door and turned away. I wasn't worried. His general build, short, like a caricatured Rumpelstiltskin, and lack of hair at the back, would be enough to identify him. I dropped the phone back in my pocket.

"The police will hear about this, Mr Jorry, and you won't be able to deny it while I have a photograph and two witnesses. I think that whatever designs you might have on parliament, you'd better put them on the back burner until after your trial."

I released the door and with a look of utter fury, he yanked it shut. His minders got into the front and drove him away.

I turned to my heroes. "Thank you, lads. Let me do my shopping and there'll be a reward for you."

Owen's face lit up. "Ooh. Southern Comfort?"

I tutted. "You're far too young. You'll get WKD at best." I went on my way to the sound of their groans ringing in my ears.

I usually did our weekly shop on Thursday, but the previous day I'd been far too busy with Eileen McCrudden's problems. I always did it alone. Well, I say always. Once a month (or thereabouts) I would bring Dennis with me. That was when we needed to restock the freezer, and since he was responsible for the disappearance of most of the food in said freezer, I felt he could carry it to the car and help me haul it into the kitchen when we got home. From there I put it away. I had to. Dennis was a genius mechanic, but his organisational skills left much to be desired, and I preferred an orderly freezer. Left to him, he would just heap everything in anywhere.

He moaned about it. Of course he did. It was one of his finest qualities; the ability to complain about almost everything other than the cost of a head gasket for his sweet little Morris Marina.

Having become the target for the nasty little Hal Jorry and his unpleasant friends, perhaps it was time I brought Dennis here more often.

Before I wheeled my trolley into the store, I rang Mandy and made a formal complaint against Jorry, and while she was happy to hear it, content to take my word and do something about it, she insisted she needed a formal statement. I promised to cut along to the station when I was through at CutCost.

As it happened, things would warm up long before then.

It took me half an hour to get round the shop (it always did) and a further ten minutes to get through the checkout queue. From there, I had to queue again at the tobacco kiosk to pay my lottery numbers, and that's when John Frogshaw and Owen Trench emerged from a back office. Both were angry, near to tears, and shouting the odds at Aidan Crompton, the assistant manager.

"We were helping a woman who was being attacked," Owen said.

"Just get out, both of you. I don't want to see you again."

In the background, I spotted Jorry looking smug and satisfied as he watched the action.

John saw me and pointed at me. "She's there. Ask her."

I left the queue, took out my phone and dialled Mandy again, reporting the incident. She promised to send a patrol car, and I approached Crompton.

"Is there a problem?" I asked.

"I don't think it's any of your concern, Mrs Capper."

"Oh, but it is." I aimed a shaking finger at Jorry and raised my voice loud enough for half the shop to hear. "That piece of scum set two of his idiot friends on me, and these two boys stepped in to prevent them kidnapping me."

Crompton floundered and Jorry made for the door, muttering, "I don't have time to listen to this—"

"Stay where you are," I ordered. "The police are

on their way." I focussed on Crompton. "Do you have CCTV covering the car park?"

"Well, yes, we do, but, er…"

"Then check it for about…" I looked at my watch. "…three fifteen. You'll find two of his people blocking my way and trying to force me into a black BMW. And I do mean force me. He was in the back seat waiting to persuade me to back off from exposing his illegal activities." I pointed at John and Owen. "Had it not been for the intervention of these two young men, you'd probably find me in hospital… or worse."

"I've heard enough of this." Jorry made for the exit again, but John and Owen stood in his way.

And then I heard to wail of a police siren and a minute later a patrol car screeched to a halt outside the doors.

It took almost an hour to sort it out. The two officers, one of whom was Sonny Scott, already the focus of an attack from a drunken politician, took statements from Jorry, who screamed 'foul' when they wouldn't let him leave, John, Owen, Crompton, and me, but what finally tipped the scales was the CCTV footage which clearly showed the two men harassing me and trying to force me into their car. Jorry denied being in the car, but John and Owen had seen him too, and along with my allegation and fuzzy photograph, it was enough to see our wannabe führer carted off to the police station.

As they prepared to leave with their suspect, I asked Sonny to tell Mandy I'd be along when I was through at CutCost. "There are other things she needs to know about Jorry and his links to Wayne Peason's death."

With them gone, I turned my attention back to the assistant manager. "It's not my job to tell you how to run your store, Aidan, but these two young men deserve a reward, not the sack. If it hadn't been for them, heaven knows what might have happened to me."

He was suitably embarrassed and contrite. "Yes. Of course. And I'll make sure they get a mention in the company newsletter. But, you see, I had a complaint from an election candidate, and I had to take it seriously."

"I don't see why. No one else bothers to listen to Jorry."

As we came away from the office, John and Owen thanked me, but I insisted the thanks were owed to them, from me, and I handed over half a dozen bottles of WKD.

Chapter Seventeen

Once home, I rang Mandy again, laid out my allegations against Jorry in respect of Wayne Peason's death, but she was too busy to deal with them.

"He's denying everything," she told me, "but your photograph, shaky as it is, and the CCTV means we have him and his pals in the frame, and I will get round to checking this Fiat, but it won't be until tomorrow at the earliest."

"You're holding him overnight?"

She was hesitant. "Unlikely. He's screaming the interview room down right now and his solicitor is bleating about your testimony and that of young Frogshaw and Trench. He'll be released under interrogation."

"Giving him the opportunity to hassle me and those two kids again."

"Shouldn't think so, Chrissy. Frogshaw senior is capable of handling any muscle Jorry sends, and he won't dare come near you, but if you want, I can sit a patrol car outside your house for the night."

I considered it for a moment. "No. Don't do that, Mandy. I'll set up a security camera to watch the house front and back, and I'll be in touch sometime tomorrow or over the weekend."

After cutting the call, I rang Eileen McCrudden and got no answer, so I rang her husband, and got no answer. In the end, I rang his works and got his sour-faced secretary.

"I can't account for Mrs McCrudden," said Rowena Benson, "but Mr McCrudden had a hospital appointment and I don't expect him back today."

Having drawn a blank, I left a message for Eileen to ring me when she was free, and then attended to the demands of Cappy the Cat who had been haggling for food since I walked in.

After putting his dish down and opening the conservatory door so he could come and go as he pleased, I put away the week's groceries, and then rang Dennis. "You won't forget I'm doing you a special dinner tonight."

"Looking forward to it, lass. Grimy's already gone. There's karaoke at the Sump Hole tonight. Geronimo's taking his missus out, so he'll be away in ten minutes, and I'll be knocking off between six and quarter past."

Remember the old adage of a woman's work is never done? I wouldn't argue with it. With the time coming up to five o'clock, I barely had time to squeeze in a cup of tea before I began work on Dennis's treat.

First I had to cook the meat, boiling it in a pan, and while that was busy, I peeled the potatoes. My pies, cooked the way my mother taught me, were not like the store bought affairs where the meat and potatoes turned to a sort of general mush inside the crust. They consisted of whole (manageable) chunks of meat and properly cooked potatoes, all in a rich gravy and covered with a thick crust, talking of which, the moment the spuds were peeled and ready, I began work on the pastry, working, kneading the plain flour, mixing it with a little milk, and some butter, working it, rolling it, working it, rolling it, until I had a thick, flat and floppy cake the size of a dinner plate, ready to cover the pie once it was in the basin and ready for shoving in the oven.

As I worked I recalled my childhood years when my brother, Stephen, and I would wait in the front room while mother prepared the same pie, and the odour of fabulous home cooking permeated the whole house to the point where we were going crazy, waiting for Dad to get home from work so we could tuck in. My two children were the same when they were that age; appetites in overdrive, going mental waiting for the feast. And one thing was for sure. There were four empty plates at the end of the meal, not a single scrap left over.

Because there were only the two of us, I used a smaller basin these days, but the outcome was just the same. Neither Dennis, Cappy the Cat, nor I left anything for the local scavengers. And if it didn't do my weight any favours, so what? You know what they say about a little bit of what you fancy. And I could always work the excess off over the weekend walking round CutCost to seek out my new kitchen.

Throughout that next hour, I was too busy to give any thought to Eileen McCrudden and her troubles, or to any grief I might have created for Hal Jorry (which he deserved) and with the time coming up to six o'clock, I put the pie in the oven, and whipped into the bathroom to take a shower. I needed it. I could never understand why, but every time I worked with flour it ended up all over my clothing, bare arms, and face, but never in my hair. The amount I paid Sonya's Unisex Hairdressers to look after my mop every month, I was careful about that.

By half past six, I was ready for Dennis. So was Cappy the Cat, or more precisely, Cappy the Cat was ready for the pie.

With no sign of him at quarter to seven, I was getting annoyed, so I rang to find out where he was and got no answer. That was unusual. Even when he was driving, Dennis would have the mobile set on hands free and he would answer.

I had visions of him bent under a bonnet, tinkering with the engine of some old car, too absorbed to leave it and answer the phone, and my anger rose. I rang again. And again. And again and again and again, and got the same result every time.

I was on the point of jumping in the car and driving down to Haxford Fixers to drag him away from there, when my phone beeped to signal an incoming message.

It was from an unknown number and when I opened it, I found a photograph. It was poor, but it looked like Haxford Fixers' workshop and one of the partners was spark out on the floor. I couldn't be certain but it looked like Dennis. But that couldn't be. Could it? I mean, why would he be…

My thoughts came to a tumbling halt. His head was matted with what looked like blood, and in his right hand, he held a length of pipe, but the hand, too, was streaked with blood.

Panic began to spread through me. He told me he was alone. If he'd had an accident, then he needed help.

Almost as I thought of it, another message arrived and it was a text this time. I opened it and read, *Don't fret. We called an ambulance. We'll do the same for you when it's your turn.*

He hadn't had an accident. He'd been attacked. It was obvious really and if I wasn't so worked up, I would have realised it. If he'd had an accident, who took the picture?

The shock hit me like a hammer and I didn't know what to do, who to call, where to go. I pulled myself together, rushed to the hall, grabbed my coat, fished out my car keys, and as I opened the door, a police patrol car pulled up outside the front gate, and two uniforms climbed out: Sonny Scott and Fliss Keele.

"Hi, Christine," said Sonny. "Can we come in a minute, luv?"

"It's Dennis, isn't it? I've had a message."

"And we'll need to see that." Sonny put on his most sympathetic face. "I'm sorry, Chrissy. It's not good news. He's a heck of a mess."

It's hard to quantify the shock. On a scale of one to ten, it was about fifteen, maybe twenty, and it took all my self-control to stop me breaking down on the doorstep. "He's dead. Isn't he?"

Sonny was too well trained to answer right away. "No, but let's talk inside, eh? Better than putting on a show for your neighbours."

I was reeling as I led them into the kitchen.

I'd known Sonny (his real name, BTW) for a few years. He was one of Simon's patrol partners before my son was made up to acting DC. He was from solid, Haxford stock, via the Caribbean, but you wouldn't think it to hear his accent. Pure Yorkshire, and he once told me he'd never been closer to Jamaica than Burnham-on-Sea, which only counted because it was in Somerset, on the west coast.

I didn't know Fliss well. A blonde in her early twenties, I had a nodding acquaintanceship with her, but I couldn't recall ever passing the time of day with her.

I made for the kettle, but Sonny guided me to the table and Fliss took over the brewing detail. It was one of those jobs I had done on any number of occasions when I was her age, in uniform, and we had bad news to deliver. Sweet tea. A remedy for shock. I don't know that there was any medical evidence to back up the claim, but it was standard procedure, especially when you were delivering the worst possible news.

"You don't have to lie, Sonny. Is he dead?"

Once again, he shushed me, declining to answer immediately until Fliss arrived with the tea, when he went into his account. "I'm not lying, Chrissy. He's still with us but he's in a bad way. Mandy Hiscoe's down at the mill now, along with your Simon and the forensic crew. When we left, the paramedics were ready for carting him off to Huddersfield Royal, but he was alive. Now you mentioned a message. Can I see it?"

I handed him my phone and sank back on my chair. I wanted to cry, but I couldn't. There would be time enough for that later. For now I had to steel myself to get through this, take in all the information I could, and yet, as I tried to sort out my jumbled thoughts, trying to drum up questions I should be asking, the most absurd thought leapt into my mind. That pie was a waste of money, energy, and time, but Cappy the Cat would reap the benefit.

I forced myself to focus. "What happened? Do you know?"

"Not really." He tapped my phone. "Looking at these messages, he was attacked, but we'd already guessed that. Odd thing though. He was on his own. There was no sign of Grimy or Geronimo." The use of my husband's partners' nicknames demonstrated how well Sonny knew his job and the people he dealt with on a day to day basis.

My head was still clogged with thoughts of Dennis lying in a hospital bed, and I had to force myself to focus, to bring them up to speed. "I spoke to Dennis just before five, and he told me that Lester left early and Tony Wharrier was ready for knocking off. He's taking his wife out tonight or something. Now, come on, Sonny. This is Christine you're taking to. Tell me what you know."

"Not much," he admitted. "He's been beaten up. Badly. Mandy will probably know more. She's leading, unless they can get Paddy Quinn down from Huddersfield, but even so she knows the crack at your Dennis's place. Haxford Fixers have CCTV don't they?"

I nodded. "I don't know whether it's working. Probably not."

"Well, there are security cameras fitted to the

outside of the mill, and when we came away, your Simon was on his way to security to chase them up. Dennis had a long piece of piping in one hand when the paramedics got to him. Well, you've seen it in the photo haven't you? Mandy figures that with a bit of luck, he might have lashed back at his attacker and caused him some injury. That might give us a lead. The place is a mess. It wasn't just Dennis they hit. They've smashed the workshop up bad."

The scenario painted itself in my fevered mind, and I almost broke down. Again, I had to steel myself. "Who reported it?"

"Dunno. Emergency services got a call from an unregistered number, and the paramedics turned up twenty minutes later, and found him as you see him in the picture. They took one look at him and the mess the place was in and rang us while they got on with the job of treating him."

"But he could be dead by now?" It was a grim thought, yes, but one way or the other, I had to know.

"Let's look on the bright side, Chrissy. He was alive. He still will be."

None of which was any comfort to me.

Sonny's phone rang. He excused himself and put it to his ear. "Yes… Right, Sarge, I'll make sure Christine knows." He ended the call. "That was Mandy. Your Simon's on his way over. Once he gets here we'll clear off."

Almost as he said it, the door opened and Naomi walked in, with Bethany hanging onto her hand, and I guessed Simon must have rung her. They only lived a few streets away.

Bethany rushed to me, shouting a delighted, "Nanna" and I hugged her. And right then, with my arms around this happy little girl, I broke down.

I couldn't help it. She was three years old, too young to understand what had happened to her grandad and the manner in which was breaking her grandma's heart. All she knew was her delight at seeing Nanna, who spoiled her at every opportunity. I envied this child's innocence. One day in the distant future she would endure trauma similar to mine, whether for an injured husband, a dead grandparent, a broken marriage, whatever, but I didn't want her to. I wanted her to stay as she was, an innocent enjoying the delights of an uncomplicated life.

I felt Naomi's arm come round my shoulder. She was the daughter I wanted but which I never found in Ingrid, the daughter who was near, needing me when she needed me, supporting me when I needed her. Ingrid had my undying love but she was fiercely independent and too far away to be with me now.

Naomi understood. She had her arm around me, but said nothing. Words were pointless. Comfort was all I needed, the comfort of someone close, someone I could rely on. And as she sat there, I cried. Self-pity, Dennis would say, and he would be half right. My oh so cosy, comfortable life had nose-dived into nightmare. But it wasn't all about me. The other angle, the one he might not grasp, was the terrible thought of what some animal (I could think of no other description) had done to the man I loved.

And I knew there would be worse to come before this terrible ordeal was over.

Simon arrived. He looked angry, and there followed a few minutes of serious, whispered debate between Sonny, Fliss and my son, before the uniformed pair left with appropriate commiserations, and I let Simon comfort me with an extended hug while I sobbed some more.

It was almost quarter to eight when we sat down to a fresh cup of tea, and he brought me up to date.

"I rang Huddersfield Royal while I was on my way over, Mam. Dad's in surgery right now. Head injuries, both legs broken, god knows how many cuts and bruises. It says something for him that he survived, and it shows you how tough he is. He was holding a length of steel pipe, and we found blood on it and we don't think it's his. Forensics have that. Mandy reckons he landed out at one of his attackers and with luck and a following wind, we'll get a DNA match." He smiled savagely at my phone in an evidence bag. Forensics would need it to track down the source of the messages. "And if we can get a track on the mobile which sent this… this crap to you, we'll nail 'em."

Under better control of myself, I said, "I don't need a DNA match or a trace on the phone. It was Jorry and his thugs. They attacked me in the car park at CutCost, and I got them to back off…with a bit of help."

"I know. Young Frogshaw and his pal, Digger Trench. I sat in on the interviews with Mandy, and Jorry denied it all. But get your police head on,

Mam. We don't know that this has anything to do with him."

"Who else? And why are you here, Simon? You should be down there helping Mandy."

He sighed. "I can't, and you know it. He's my father, and that automatically bars me from the investigation."

I knew it all right, but the distress and fury rumbling inside me clouded my thinking. I dragged myself to my feet. "I'd better get to Huddersfield."

My son put his foot down with the same force as I used to when he was a boy. "No way. Forget it, Mam. I'm not letting you drive to Huddersfield like that."

"Use your loaf, Simon," Naomi insisted. "Chrissy needs to see Dennis. You take her. I'll stay here, mind the store for you and look after Cappy the Cat, Chrissy."

I didn't want to put them out like that, but Naomi insisted and I agreed with a silent nod.

Simon agreed. "I'll bell Mandy and get her to station a patrol car outside." He smiled. "Just in case they decide to try again."

Chapter Eighteen

It was getting dark when we pulled out of Bracken Close at twenty past eight. Huddersfield Royal was on the far side of the town from Haxford, and it would take at least thirty to forty minutes to get there.

Simon rang them before we left, only to be told that Dennis was still in theatre, and they couldn't say when he would be out or whether we would be allowed anywhere near him. I insisted I wanted to be there anyway, and Simon stood by me.

I was dreading it. I didn't know what damage might have been done to Dennis, so I didn't know what to expect other than a man unconscious, unable to hear me, unable to accept my love.

As we drove along I thought back on the last couple of days and wished I'd never heard of Eileen McCrudden and her rotten blackmail problems, never got involved with the would-be politicians, men and women prepared to sponsor this kind of senseless thuggery to protect their precious reputations. And as for Hal Jorry... for his own safety, he would be well advised not to come within reach of me.

It was all a distraction. It kept me away from the dread of what lay ahead of us, anything from a man wired into all sorts of electronic jiggery-pokery, to one in a permanent vegetative state and a medical team waiting for my agreement to switch off his life support.

How could this happen? Three hours ago, I was busy in the kitchen, preparing a meal as a treat to put right the squabble between us, and now I was an anxious wreck, the cosy fabric of my comfortable life left in smithereens.

When people spoke of life-changing events, they talked in terms of winning the lottery jackpot, or landing a promotion which guaranteed them a rosy future. But what of the other side of the coin? A bad traffic accident, a cancer diagnosis, a heart condition discovered, even a long term relationship coming to an end? Didn't they change lives too? What happened to Dennis was such a moment. It didn't matter whether he recovered in a week, a month or a year, our life, so comfortable, so secure, so contented, would never be the same.

The hospital car park was almost full, but Simon parked where he could find a space and left his official police notice in the front windscreen. Almost as we climbed out of the car, a security officer challenged him, but he flashed his warrant card and the man backed off.

We made our way into A&E, where face masks, a hangover from the coronavirus pandemic, were still compulsory, and while I sat nearby, he spoke to the woman behind the glass, and we were directed to the urgent treatment waiting area, where, once again, he spoke to a senior triage nurse, who came back and reported that Dennis was out of theatre, in recovery, and they were waiting for news.

We were surprised at nine o'clock when DI Paddy Quinn paid us a visit. Normally, Paddy and I got on like electricity and water, a mixture that could be lethal, but for once, he displayed the patience and understanding of a saint. After taking a brief, verbal report from Simon, which confirmed the details he'd already had from Mandy, he turned his attention to me.

"I understand your concern for Dennis, Christine, so I won't give you any earache, but you have my personal assurance that we will spare no effort to find these scum and bring them to heel. I would ask you not to interfere. I know you're a private investigator and you're bound to want to push for information, but it's obvious from what we've learned – and I know that's not much – and from the messages you received that these people will not hesitate to attack you the way they've assaulted your husband, and it's bad enough seeing Dennis in here without you joining him."

"Thank you, Patrick." I felt obliged to use his full name. "I know who it is, even if you, Mandy, and Simon won't have it, but I doubt that I'll have much time for ferreting around. I will speak to Tony and Lester and whatever information I get, I'll make sure it comes straight to you via either Simon or Mandy."

"Me or Mandy," he corrected me. "I'm sorry, Simon, but Dennis is your father, and you can't be allowed to take any active part in the investigation. You can work on the periphery; admin and the like, but you mustn't get involved."

"I understand, sir."

Quinn left half an hour later, and soon after, my son and I were directed to the High Dependency Unit. Once there, the ward manager guided us to a small waiting room, and for the third time, I sat, trying to quell my rising anxiety.

A few minutes later, Dr Kassim, a pleasantly spoken man somewhere in his mid to late thirties, joined us. He looked tired, drawn, in need of a good night's sleep, but he persevered, speaking first to Simon.

"I understand you're a police officer. If you're waiting to speak to Mr Capper, you've a—"

"I'm also Mr Capper's son." Simon handed over his warrant card for Kassim to examine it. "I didn't want to risk my mother driving all the way here. She's in a bit of a state, as you can imagine."

"Ah. Of course. A wise decision, Mr Capper." Kassim beamed a benign smile upon me. "I'll pull no punches, madam, your husband has been seriously injured."

"But he will recover?"

"It's too early to talk about that. He survived and that is the main thing for the moment."

Determined not to evade the issues, because he knew I would not want to, Simon pressed for more information. "The extent of his injuries, Doc?"

"Multiple cuts and contusions, right tibia, broken, left femur, broken. Bones in both legs are immobilised and surgery was not necessary. He was wearing heavy duty overalls when he came in, we believe those saved his legs from more serious damage. His major injury, however, is a depressed skull fracture. We operated in order to lift the fragments, and prevent them from pressing on the brain. It is this which most concerns us. I'm sorry to say that the extent of recovery is often in the lap of the gods, and until he properly regains consciousness, we have no idea how it might affect him. Even then, the complications arising from two broken legs may result in a considerable wait before we know how it affects matters such as balance and coordination. I'm sorry to have to say this, Mrs Capper, but you are in for a long, and potentially difficult road ahead. Have you been married long?"

"Twenty-eight years." The tears began to form in my eyes. "Twenty-eight happy years."

Simon took my hand and squeezed it gently. "We'll get him there, Mam. Nam and I are only a couple of streets away, remember, and we'll be there to help whenever you need us."

I was so distressed I forgot to remind him not to call his wife 'Nam'.

Kassim took up the tale once more. "At the moment, your husband is heavily sedated, and we will wean him off the sedatives over the course of the coming days. Without them, he would be in intolerable pain. Once his bones heal – and that may take time – he will need physiotherapy to restore the strength in both legs. As for the potential for brain injury…" He shrugged. "We do not know. That will be a matter of time and patience. And I'm sorry, but I cannot give you any better news than that."

"Can I see him?"

"Of course. It's a sterile area, so you will need protective aprons and gloves, but you can sit with him for a little while. I must warn you, Mrs Capper, he is not a pretty sight, and of course, he cannot communicate with you."

I pulled myself together. "I used to be a police officer, Doctor. Like my son. I'm sure I can cope."

But I couldn't. The moment I saw him, my heart broke and I fell into Simon's arms once more and sobbed and wept and sobbed and wept.

Dennis was flat on his back, a cage lifting the bed linen away from his damaged legs, and as I anticipated, he was wired into every system in the hospital. A tangle of cables and tubes straggling down from various bits of machinery, some of which I knew about, most of which I hadn't a clue.

His eyes were closed and his head was wrapped in bandages. His jaw was swollen where he had ridden a punch. One eye was bruised and blackened, and both hands, resting on the uppermost linen, were grazed, streaked with the dried blood I'd seen on the shocking photograph and which the medics had tried to clean up.

I sat alongside him, tears streaming down my face and soaking my facemask. I took hold of his hand, and then lost myself to the memories of the last three decades.

I was twenty-two when we met, Dennis was twenty-one, and back then he wasn't quite as obsessed with motor cars. He was into Madonna and Kylie and I was in love with Jason Donavan, Jive Bunny, Simply Red. We began dating, then we were going steady, and then we decided to move in together. We stayed that way for two years, until the day I announced I was pregnant with the young detective constable sat alongside me. We were married four months later, and I became Christine Capper instead of Christine Fordice.

Since then we had the same ups and downs as any other couple; straining to meet the mortgage, kitting out two children with school uniforms, arguing with those two children when they wanted the freedom of adulthood while they were still in their early teens. I recalled the worry surrounding Dennis's redundancy from Addison's and the bigger worries associated with setting up a new business. I recalled my pride when Simon went off to university and Dennis's disappointment when Simon wouldn't consider a career at Haxford Fixers, but I also remembered the way Dennis would talk to people and the manner in which he always mentioned his son. "He's at university you know." He might have been irked at Simon's refusal to join Haxford Fixers, but he was secretly just as proud as me.

Sitting there, holding his hand, quietly crying to myself, I remembered the holidays we had enjoyed over the years. Scarborough, Blackpool, Torquay, St Ives, then daring to fly off to warmer climes; the Spanish Costas, the Balearics, the Canary Islands, the Greek Islands, Cyprus, Malta, Turkey, even America. I remembered how nervous we were that first time on an aeroplane and how, over the years, it became almost second nature to us; just like getting on a bus.

Images of the different cars we had owned came into my mind; from clapped out Ford Escorts, hangovers of the early eighties, to my sweet little

Renault, which even if it was getting a year or two on its back, we bought brand new.

Thirty years. Three decades of memories rolled from the depths of my mind, and flooded my tired, frightened, distressed consciousness. Arguing, falling out, making up, making love as eagerly as rabbits, then more patiently, more indulgent, more satisfying.

We were not old. Middle-aged by some definitions, but give Dennis an engine, and he was a boy again, playing with a live Meccano set. Give me a puzzle, something to distract my eager mind, and I was a young girl, filled with a yearning for life in the fast lane.

He could be tough when he had to be, but he had always been gentle as a lamb with me, and for all his hard head, I recalled him crying like a child when his father passed away.

Thirty, normal and happy years. Twenty-eight of them in matrimony, all taken away by a wannabe word merchant and his mindless thugs.

"You'd better get to Jorry before me, Simon, or I swear I will kill him."

Chapter Nineteen

The news broke on Saturday morning but being the weekend, most people had too much to do for it to impinge on their consciousness. The neighbours soon learned and rallied round. If there was anything they could do to help, all I had to do was shout. Lester and Tony rang the house phone after being unable to get through to me. They couldn't, could they? My mobile was with the police. They were both consumed with guilt as much as sadness. If only they hadn't gone home early... Simon rang Ingrid and she paid a flying visit on Saturday afternoon, had a weep at her father's bedside, spent another hour with me, but had to go back to Scarborough. She had a gig on that night, but she promised to visit again during the week and she would ring every day. I wouldn't hold my breath for that second visit. She and her partner were contracted to work on a holiday park for the season, and getting time off on any day other than Saturday (changeover day) was difficult, but I knew she would ring.

Mandy returned my phone at noon on Saturday and told me that the police were keeping things low key over the weekend. It was always the same with any investigation. They gave a brief, factual statement to the press, saying Dennis was hospitalised after an assault, but nothing more.

I knew what was happening, but Mandy kept me up to speed anyway. Having taken the information from my smartphone, they were trying to trace the unregistered mobile from which the image and message had been sent. That could be a long haul and might not come to anything. Haxford Fixers' CCTV was (as I guessed) inoperative. The cameras were on, sure, but they were not recording anything. The police had secured footage from the mill's security control, and when Mandy called on Saturday, she assured me that Huddersfield CID were working on it in an attempt to identify who might have been responsible.

I maintained my insistence that it was Jorry and his bully boys, but Mandy and Simon persuaded me to keep away from it, at least for the time being, and I agreed. It left me with nothing better to do than visit with Dennis, and I spent hours at his bedside during Saturday afternoon and evening, holding his hand, talking to him between bouts of crying, waiting for him to wake up while the nurses comforted me.

I wasn't there when it eventually happened. In the early hours of Sunday morning, he came round, and the ward rang me at ten in the morning to deliver the good news. But it was not all sweetness and light. When I visited on Sunday afternoon, he could barely speak and the whispered sounds coming from him were unintelligible. Worse than that, he did not recognise me, and he wasn't sure who he was. All he knew for certain was that his name was Dennis, and he only knew that because the nurses called him by his given name.

"It's not unusual, Mrs Capper," the young female doctor managing his case assured me. "Concussion resulting from skull fractures can lead to what's known as traumatic brain injury –TBI for short – and that often leads to post-traumatic amnesia, which can last for hours, days, weeks, and in some cases, months." Then she reiterated what Dr Kassim had told me on Friday night. "We're not saying that's the case with Dennis, but as you know, we're monitoring him twenty-four-seven. He's a strong man, and we're confident that he'll make a full recovery, but you should be prepared for months of rehabilitation."

That presented other, more immediate problems, associated with Haxford Fixers, and to some extent, my work on Eileen McCrudden's case.

I rang Eileen late on Sunday afternoon and gave her a brief account of what had happened. She was (politically) contrite.

"I am so sorry, Christine, but it does make my mind up for me. I will retire from the election, and if you prepare your final account, I'll ensure that it's paid immediately."

The announcement forced my irritation to the surface, temporarily displacing the anxiety. "It's not that simple, Eileen. This was a violent attack designed to persuade me to back off, and I know who was behind it. Once the police move and arrest Hal Jorry—"

"Jorry?" Surprise bordering on astonishment.

"He attacked me earlier in the day and when that

failed, when I reported him to the police, he was questioned and had to back off from me, so he targeted my husband instead. As I was saying, once the police arrest him again, everything will come out, including my work on your behalf, which was his motive. He wanted to stop me exposing him as a blackmailer. I'll send you my final bill, of course, but you should prepare yourself for a rough ride."

"Oh lord, I wish I'd never started this."

I felt it would have been better if she'd kept her knickers on ten years ago, but I refrained from saying so, and rang off promising to keep her up to date on events.

I arranged to meet with Tony and Lester at the workshop on Monday morning. Aside from having to put the place to rights, they would need a replacement mechanic. Both agreed to meet me at ten o'clock, but in the relative comfort of Sandra's Snacky.

Events would move much faster than that, starting with the arrest of Hal Jorry first thing Monday morning, and at a few minutes to nine, Paddy Quinn put in an appearance on local TV news.

"On Friday night, Mr Dennis Capper, one of Haxford's most respected local businessmen, was attacked in his workshop. During the course of the assault, Mr Capper suffered severe injuries, including a depressed skull fracture and two broken legs. He survived and is currently under the care of Huddersfield Royal Infirmary, where medical staff have advised us that his recovery is likely to take many months. After studying CCTV from Haxford

Mill security cameras, we are seeking to interview Bernard Singleton and Peter Nesbitt, two men known to have attacked Mr Capper's wife, Christine, earlier in the day. Singleton and Nesbitt are known associates of Mr Harold Jorry, and we have brought Mr Jorry in under suspicion of involvement in the attack. The public are advised to keep their distance from these two men. They are considered violent and unpredictable. Anyone spotting them or anyone who knows of their whereabouts should contact their local police immediately."

All right, so he wasn't exactly a candidate for taking over the BBC's ten o'clock news, but he got the message across, and as at the hospital on Friday evening, he was quite polite when referring to Dennis and me.

Within minutes of his appearance the phones started to ring, both the landline and my smartphone, and they would not stop for most of the morning and into the afternoon.

First it was Val Wharrier, Tony's wife, offering her commiserations, then it was Reggie Monk asking after Dennis, and reassuring me that if I couldn't make my debut broadcast on Tuesday it wouldn't be a problem. I said I would let him know. The newsdesk at the Haxford Recorder rang asking for quotes, but I declined, telling them that my concern was my husband, and I was leaving the police to deal with the criminal side of things. Keith McCrudden rang as I was ready to leave the house, but all he could say was, "I'm so sorry, dear lady." After him, as I was climbing into the car, it was

Sandra Limpkin from the Snacky, asking after one of her favourite customers, and reassuring me that Dennis and I had her full support for the future. Half a dozen others rang while I was driving to the mill, but I left them to my voicemail. Amongst them were people like Benny Barnes, who had suffered a similar, but not nearly so devastating attack in his shop the previous Christmas, Sonya, from the hairdresser's, and even the proprietors of Pottle's Pet Supplies, who regularly sponsored my vlog. Terry from the market hall tea bar rang to offer his commiserations, but the most surprising call came as I parked outside Haxford Fixers' workshop. It was from Ambrose Davenport.

"I rang to offer my sympathies, Mrs Capper, and please convey my best wishes to your husband. I hope he recovers soon. Our meeting on Friday was quite, er, acerbic, but no matter what our political differences, I don't hold with violence, and if Mr Jorry is involved then I would expect the law to deal with him accordingly."

I thanked him, ended the call and walked into the workshop where Lester and Tony were completing the job of tidying up. It didn't look as bad as Sonny Scott had led me to believe, but then, I didn't know how long Dennis's partners had been about the job of putting it right.

They locked up and we made our way to the third floor and Sandra's Snacky, where the woman herself presented the two men with a full breakfast, and supplied me with tea and toast, all of it, "on the house. And when you get these scroats, bring 'em here. I'll show 'em what real blood-letting is all about. I've a meat knife here, and it's sharp enough to cut off their—"

"Yes, thank you, Sandra. We get the picture."

"Just make sure you give Dennis a kiss from me and tell him I wanna see him back in here the week after next."

I doubted that Dennis would even remember who she was, but I didn't say so. Instead, I got down to brass tacks with the two thirds of Haxford Fixers still operational.

Lester was known for his lackadaisical, laid back attitude, and under normal circumstances, he mixed it with saucy innuendo, usually aimed at me, but now he was deadly serious. Well, as serious as Lester Grimes was ever likely to be. "Geronimo's more up to snuff with the accounts and stuff, Chrissy, but the diary's full. We've got folk out there waiting to bring their motors in for service and pre-MOT examinations. I mean, I can do some of it, but I'm nowhere near as good with the spanners as your Cappy. Do we know how long he'll be laid up?"

"Not precisely, but the doctors are talking months rather than weeks." I turned to the third partner. "Tony?"

"Lester's got it right, Christine." He was always more formal and polite than either Lester or Dennis. "We're going to lose a lot of business unless we can bring someone in quickly. Like Lester, I can take over some of the mechanical work, but as you know, I'm a bodywork specialist, and I don't have Dennis's diagnostic skills." He tutted as he tucked into his breakfast. "He's a one off, your husband, you know. They broke the mould after they made Dennis. He can lean on the bonnet of your car while the engine's running and tell you what's wrong with it, and it's not often that he's wrong."

It was something I had always been aware of, albeit on a subliminal level. "So is there any problem with bringing in another mechanic?"

"I've already rung the Job Centre," Tony said, "and it's a case of waiting to see who bites, but it won't be cheap. And, of course, you have other problems, don't you? Aside from Dennis getting better, that is."

If we did, I hadn't had time to think about them. "Such as?"

"Money," said Lester, as he pushed his breakfast plate away. "See, lass, the way we work here, we all take a set amount out of the work we do in our inder-vid-oo-al capacities. Eighty percent. And what's left over goes to pay the rent, electric, and stuff. Then whatever we have at the end of every quarter, we divvy up three ways. I mean it's a good dip, don't get me wrong, but your Dennis won't be doing any work, and we'll have this grease monkey to pay, so you and your old man are gonna take a hit until Cappy can get back to work."

I was wrong. I had thought about it, but I'd pushed it to the back of my mind. I had more to worry about. "Dennis has income protection insurance," I said.

"As do I," Tony assured me. "It kicks in after one month – I think – and it'll pay him fifty or sixty percent of his usual income, but only for one year. Will he recover by then?"

"I would hope so, but I really don't know."

Lester was not about to let Tony steal the moment. "Well, me and Geronimo talked about this, Chrissy, and what we'll do is this. When it comes to the quarterly divvy, we'll take a quarter instead of a third, and let you and Cappy have the other half. It won't make you much better off, but it'll help."

I could feel the tears welling up again, and I was bursting with love for these two men, whom I'd known for years, and whose respect for Dennis had never been spelled out so clearly.

"Thank you. Both of you, but let's put that on hold for the time being, see how Dennis and I get on. Now, how will you manage to pay for a mechanic?"

"We won't put him on the books," Tony said. "We'll take him on but only on a self-employed basis. He'll be paid whatever he makes, minus twenty percent." He frowned. "Even so, I can see customers deserting us, and it'll probably take some time to get it together when Dennis gets back to work."

Lester gave me a toothless grin. "In the meantime, Chrissy, if you get strapped for cash and you decided to start selling yourself, I'm first in line."

Now that was more like the Lester Grimes I knew.

***

From the mill I made my way down into town and the police station. I wanted an update from Mandy. As always, my timing was anything but impeccable.

As I walked into reception, Jorry was making his way out with his solicitor. The red mist rose and for the only time in my life that I could remember, I lost the plot completely and launched myself at him.

"You almost killed my husband, you slimy toe rag."

My foot connected with his shin. Like the overweight coward that he really was, he scurried away, limping back into a corner, and I followed him. His solicitor grabbed my arm, I shrugged him off, and attacked Jorry again, this time with my fists as well as my feet.

"Get her off me." His cry was the wail of a child terrified for its safety. "Get her off me."

I felt hands upon me, but this time, it wasn't the solicitor. It was Simon, Sonny Scott, and Fliss Keele. Determined to get to Jorry, I tried to fight them off, and I heard Mandy's urgent voice in the background.

"Get Chrissy out of here. Take her to the canteen."

While they dragged me away, my eyes still on Jorry, my voice, unrecognisable even to me, spitting curses at him, I heard the solicitor protest.

"My client is innocent, Sergeant, and this is not good enough. I will be reporting the matter."

"You do that, and you know how much action we're likely to take. Now do us all a favour, and get that scum out of my sight."

Chapter Twenty

I was in serious trouble. The disgraceful farce downstairs constituted assault. I had assaulted Hal Jorry.

Fortunately, while there were any number of witnesses, they were all police officers, all known to me, and with the exception of Jorry's solicitor, all in my corner. It would be Mandy's job to report the incident and recommend any action the police might take.

Fliss stayed with me in the canteen, secured a cup of tea, and with a noticeable delicacy of tact, chattered about the poor weather, the state of television, Haxford Women's football team, anything, everything, but not what had happened in reception.

Mandy joined us after a few minutes. She was furious, and the target of her anger was me. She got herself a cup of tea, dismissed Fliss, and sat facing me. I opened my mouth to speak, but she held a hand to shut me up before I could say a word.

"I don't want to hear it, Chrissy. You should know better. You used to be one of us, and you know I can't ignore this. If his solicitor hadn't been there, fair enough, but he witnessed it, and I've no choice but to report you for assault. I'll have a word with the Super, and considering the state of your mind, the injuries to Dennis, and all the rest of it, I'm sure he'll recommend nothing more than a caution, but remember, it'll go on record."

I began to cry again. "I'm sorry, Mandy. I saw him, thought of Dennis, and I just lost it."

"The problem is, Chrissy, he had little or nothing to do with what happened to Dennis."

The shock choked off my tears and almost made me spill my tea. "Rubbish. Paddy Quinn said on TV this morning that you were looking for Singleton and Nesbitt. They're the pair who had a go at me in the supermarket car park. They work for him. He was in their car, for God's sake."

"Yes, I know, and we have him bang to rights on that. And I'm with you. I believe he pushed those two to hit Dennis, but he was nowhere near the mill at the time, and we know that for certain. He was in full view of dozens of people at a rally on the open market. We have him on video, and he was already busy slagging us off, accusing us of harassing him to minimise his election prospects. We dragged him in again at seven this morning, put him under pressure, and he identified Singleton and Nesbitt as the two clowns who hassled you at CutCost."

"But the phone messages—"

"Not his phone. Not registered, so it probably belongs to one of the other two."

I felt my frustration mounting. "And you haven't got them yet?"

"No. But we do have an All Ports Warning out on them." She was beginning to cool down, and went on in friendlier terms. "I know how upset you are, Chrissy, I know what this business is doing to you, but chill out. Back off. You look after Dennis and let us deal with this."

I stared into my cup. I had never felt so down. Dennis laid up in hospital, Haxford Fixers facing problems, and now me, guilty of assault and reported for it. How much worse could things get?

I looked up. "Wayne Peason. You must have Jorry for that. The damage to his car—"

Mandy let out a frustrated sigh to interrupt me. "You're doing it again. You've got Jorry on the brain. It wasn't him, Chrissy. We got paint samples from Wayne's body. We haven't identified them properly, but we do know that they didn't come from a white Fiat 500. They were from a black car."

I seized on the admission. "His thugs use a black BMW."

"Yes, we know, but we're certain the paint doesn't come from a Beamer, either. Whoever ran Wayne down, it wasn't Jorry or his goons." She took a swallow of tea to help calm her down. "The way we see it is this. You hassled Jorry at the college on Friday, and let slip that you were investigating blackmail against one of his election opponents. He must have had an inkling because he rang you on the radio, but he wanted more information, and that's why he hassled you on the car park at CutCost. When you reported him and his pals, he decided it was good, political capital. It gave him the opportunity to shoot his mouth off on the market later that evening. Singleton and Nesbitt didn't see it like that. They were looking at the possibility of doing time for hassling you, so they took it upon themselves to smash Dennis on Friday night. CCTV shows their car sat outside the workshop for a while, waiting for Grimy and Geronimo to leave, and when they knew Dennis was alone then they went in and gave him a good hiding as a warning to you. We'll get them, Chrissy, but you have to accept, that until we can demonstrate otherwise, Jorry had nothing to do with any of this. Yes, he's a dipstick, and we're sure he put Singleton and Nesbitt up to the assaults, but unless those two finger him he'll walk away from it. Think about it. If the incident downstairs tells you anything, it's that he's a born coward. I saw his face when you were thumping him. He was terrified. Chances are that all he wanted at CutCost yesterday was to talk to you and he needed backup to do that. You've come across scores of men like him in your time. All mouth and no bottle. The minute you stand up to them, they turn and run."

If I felt the pressure before, it was even worse now. How could I have got it so wrong? I had made one of the most basic mistakes any investigator could make. I let appearances, a mask mislead me. But if it wasn't Jorry, who was it?

"The paint samples from the car which ran Wayne down. You haven't had the proper analysis yet?"

"Later today with a bit of luck. Tomorrow at the latest. Now do us all a favour, Chrissy, and do like I say. Concentrate on Dennis. Concentrate on getting him home and looking after him. Whatever comes out of all this, we'll deal with it."

"I promise."

"How's he's doing?"

I felt the tears forming yet again. "Not good. Both legs broken, injuries to his neck, arms, hands, a fractured skull. He still hasn't worked out who I am, and he's not sure who he is. If he's making the right kind of progress, they'll probably discharge him later in the week. Even so, the medics reckon it'll be months before I get him back properly."

She shook her head and looked as downcast as I felt. "I'm really sorry, kid. I know Dennis can be a bit vague, and he's totally obsessed with motors, but underneath it all, he's a hell of a nice guy. He didn't deserve what happened to him and neither did you, but I'm thankful that it wasn't you. Now keep away from it. Please." She reached across the table and took my hand, and as she did so, she glanced around the canteen to make sure no one was paying any particular attention. "I can't stand to see you like this, Chrissy, so I won't report this business to the Super. If he asks, I'll tell him I've dealt with it. But as far as Jorry and his lawyer are concerned, you've had a formal caution. All right?"

I pulled in a shuddery breath. "It's more than I deserve."

For the first time since she joined me, she smiled. "Now there, I'd agree."

I came out into weak sunshine trying to fight its way through clouds as turbulent as my insides. I got into my car, but before driving away, I rang Eileen McCrudden and told her of the police conclusions that Wayne's death had nothing to do with Jorry, and logically, it meant that he was clear of the blackmail too.

After speaking to her, I rang the hospital to check on Dennis's progress, and it was the usual report. He'd had a comfortable, stable night, but he was still vague and incoherent. Promising that I would be along to see him at two o'clock, I ended the call, started the car, and drove out of the police station, making for the market car park. Once parked, I made my way through the streets to the library, where Kim greeted me with a hug and asked after Dennis.

Leaving Alden to man the counter, we retired to the little restroom, I declined tea on the grounds that I'd just drunk one with Mandy, and brought her up to date on what I knew so far.

"So if it wasn't Jorry, and it wasn't none of the other candidates, who ran him down?"

"That's the sixty-four thousand dollar question, Kim. He was Eileen McCrudden's bedmate all those years ago, and he did write those letters. I'm sure of it. But I don't think it was him making the demands."

She agreed. "If it had been Wayne, he would be asking for money. He wouldn't give a toss whether she stood in the election or not. He would have been chasing the loot."

"I worked that out a couple of days ago, and as I see it, he must have sold the information to someone else. Jorry was favourite, but enough's happened since then to dissuade me." I sighed. "It's irrelevant now anyway. The McCrudden woman has decided she's standing down."

"She's a Tory. She had no chance of winning anyway."

"That's not the point, Kim. She's been pressured into this situation, and that is a crime." I allowed my mind to wander over the possibilities again. "Tell me something. Wayne was knocked down at some time between half past one and two in the morning. Where would he have been to be coming home at that hour? And don't tell me Huddersfield. I refuse to believe he walked all the way from Huddersfield to Haxford."

"Well, if we're talking Haxford and nowhere else, it would have to be Jumping Jacks. Why? Is it important?"

"It could be. Did he meet his killer in there? Was he meeting his contact? You know, the bod who bought the information from him in the first place?"

"Only thing you can do, is go there and ask, but he wasn't forced to be there. Think about it, Chrissy. He could have bought a day saver on the bus and caught the last bus back from Huddersfield. He didn't have to be in Jumping Jacks."

I looked down my nose at her. "The last bus from Huddersfield gets in just before midnight. Use your loaf. What was he doing between midnight and half past one in the morning?"

Kim tittered. "Knowing Wayne, he could have been doing what comes naturally with some woman he'd picked up in Huddersfield." Her humour dissipated. "Never mind Wayne flaming Peason. Leave it to the cops. Now how's Dennis? I cried when I saw Paddy Quinn on the telly this morning."

I gave her the same report I had given Mandy, we left the library and walked over to the market. It was coming up to noon and I had several calls to make, the first of which was to Radio Haxford.

Reggie had finished his morning stint when a security man led me into the office. He came out of his enclosed little studio, and gave me a hug. Given his body odour, I could have lived without it, but I had to accept that the sympathy of almost every person in Haxford was coming my way.

We spent a few minutes talking, and as with Kim and Mandy, I brought him up to date on Dennis's condition, and reassured him that I would be there on Tuesday morning, and he reminded me that I would need to turn up half an hour before my slot so the office crew could brief me on the way the system worked.

"You could give it a miss, Chrissy," he assured me.

I disagreed. "Dennis won't be coming home until sometime later in the week, possibly next week, and the distraction will be good for me."

"As long as you're sure, but remember, you can't get personal on these slots. No slagging off these scroats who attacked Dennis. Ha-ha-ha"

"I won't. I'll reserve personal opinions for my vlog."

From there I called at a fruit stall, bought oranges and the traditional grapes for Dennis, then went along to the newsstand, where I picked up a couple of automotive magazines. I hadn't the faintest idea whether he was capable of understanding them, but the doctors had assured me that he needed something which might remind him of the life he had temporarily forgotten.

Finally, with the time at half past twelve, I went

to Terry's Tea Bar, ordered a cheese and tomato sandwich and a cup of tea, and tucked myself into a table at the rear, where I could eat in peace, and try to sort out my turgid thoughts.

No such luck. From the moment I sat down, various people, some of whom I didn't know, stopped by to offer their sympathies, and Terry himself spent several minutes with me, asking after Dennis, and reassuring me that if I needed help of any description, all I had to do was call.

It was turned one o'clock when I got back to the car, and sat in silence for some time, trying yet again, to sort out my thoughts.

When you train as a private investigator, one of the things they drill into you is the need to take notes. It was exactly the same in the police, and in both cases, it was the one thing I didn't do with any semblance of consistency. Right at that moment, trying to sort out my embattled emotions, and seeking some insight into Wayne Peason's death and as a consequence, Eileen McCrudden's blackmail problems, I could have done with a full notebook. Something to point me in a specific direction.

Nothing came to mind, so I started the engine, and set off on the forty minute journey to Lindley, and Huddersfield Royal Infirmary.

When I got there, Dennis was out of it on analgesics, so all I could do was sit at his bedside and read some of the magazines I had bought for him. They made little sense to me, and my big fear was they would mean nothing to him when he woke and looked through them.

I eventually left at half past four. He had not woken while I was there, and I saw no point waiting for the present round of sedation to wear off. Besides, I had more to think about and I couldn't do it in a hospital high dependency unit.

Chapter Twenty-One

After a lonely and largely sleepless night, I awoke at nine on Tuesday morning to the noise of the doorbell chiming. It was Simon.

When I got home the previous afternoon, I noticed the patrol car at the end of the drive was conspicuous by its absence, which could mean only one thing, and a call to Mandy confirmed it.

"Singleton and Nesbitt. We got 'em. The North Wales police nicked 'em on their way to Holyhead, probably chancing a boat to Ireland. Would you believe, the berks left that phone on? The one they used to send the picture and message to you. We got a GPS track on it and the North Wales boys picked them up. They'll be with us later this morning."

Tony Wharrier had news the previous evening, too. He had persuaded an old colleague, Greg Vetch to fill in for Dennis for the foreseeable future. I didn't know the man, but Tony told me he was a colleague of theirs from Addison's who had been made redundant at the same time as Dennis and Tony and had decided on an easier life in security, manning the door and looking out for shoplifters at a town centre department store.

"Where he got the idea that such work was easier than turning the spanners, we'll never know," Tony concluded.

None of which explained why Simon was ringing the doorbell to get me out of bed so early.

Panic took hold of me. Dennis. He had deteriorated overnight. He had given up the fight during the night. I was now a widow.

Even Cappy the Cat was startled by the speed and suddenness with which I jumped out of bed and hurried to the front door.

Simon stared at me then looked away. "For God's sake, put some clothes on, Mother."

I was only 'Mother' when he was annoyed with me or shocked at something I'd done. It was then that I realised I was wearing only a thin nightie, and the chilly, morning air made my nipples show through. I didn't care. I was too far gone for modesty. "What is it, Simon? Your dad? Is he—"

"Is it heck as like Dad. I've some forms for you to fill in. Now for crying out loud, put some clobber on before the neighbours start selling the pictures online and you end up as MILF of the week."

"Oh. Right." I folded my arms to hide the offending protuberances. "What's a MILF?"

"Trust me, you don't want to know."

I backed into the house, allowed him to shut and lock the front door, and while he made for the kitchen, I nipped into the bedroom and put on a thin, pink dressing gown. It was no thicker than the nightie, but the material was heavier and not so transparent, which would save my boy's blushes.

When I got to the kitchen, he was making tea for the two of us. Cappy the Cat paid a quick visit, realised it was Simon and headed for the conservatory door where I let him out. Our moody moggie had never cared for Dennis and he could take or leave Simon, but he was convinced that neither man would stop to feed him.

"So what are these forms?" I asked.

He sat with me. "Criminal injuries compensation."

"But it's too early, and we don't know whether we'll be entitled."

"I'm sure you will. So is Mandy. All I need is your signature, Mam, and I'll deal with the rest. Paddy and Mandy are planning on grilling Singleton and Nesbitt this morning, and Mandy reckons we'll have 'em charged by dinner time. And if they start blabbing, we should have Jorry back in the nick before the day's out."

He laid the form on the table, pointed to the signature box and I scrawled my name into it, then spelled it out in capital letters.

"I'll date it as appropriate, Mam." He put the form back in his briefcase. "How was Dad when you saw him yesterday?"

"Out of it. I spent a couple of hours with him, and he never woke up. They say it's the sedation, the, wotchacallems, painkillers, analgesics, but I'll admit it, Simon, I'm frightened. Suppose he's like this forever?"

"We'll cope, Mam." He cradled his beaker in his hands. "Crikey, when I think back to when me and Ingrid were kids, you were always the one who had to cope. Remember when I fell of my bike and broke my wrist? I was only about ten or eleven. Dad didn't have a clue. He was going to strap it up and send me to school. You were the one who sorted a sling out and then took me to A&E at The Cottage."

I remembered the incident like it was yesterday. While Dennis floundered, I cut up an old pillow slip, fashioned it into a makeshift sling, then left my other half to take Ingrid to school while I put Simon in the car and drove him to Haxford Cottage Hospital where they fixed him up.

It was one of those memories from our years together, memories which I hoped Dennis would be able to access again. It brought another lump to my throat.

Simon was still talking. "Whatever happens with him, you'll cope, and me and Nam are only a couple of hundred yards away, aren't we?"

"Her name is Naomi."

"That's more like my mam," he chuckled. "And she hates her name. She prefers Nam." He drained his beaker. "I'd better get going. If I get finished early, me and Nam were thinking of going to the hospital tonight to see him."

"As long as you don't expect miracles, luv." I stood, pecked him on the cheek and he took his leave of me.

When he left, the awesome loneliness crowded in on me again. We had lived in this house since before we were married, and yet, it felt like an alien environment. Dennis usually left for work at about half past seven, so I was always alone at this time of day, but now it was worse. Under normal circumstances he was a phone call away, and if I was bored or I needed information for a case, I would call at the mill and share a cup of tea with him in the Snacky. I couldn't do either right now and the silence and solitude were beginning to take their toll on me.

I had no case, either. Eileen had called it a day. Ready to stand down, she was waiting for my final bill, and that would be the end of it. That invoice would take me ten or fifteen minutes to prepare and email to her. Case closed. No conclusion, no outcome other than a badly injured husband and a life suddenly turned sour.

I could always script my weekly vlog, which was due for recording the following day, but my thought processes were such a tumult that I hadn't decided on a topic, let alone considered my approach.

It looked, therefore, like a morning mooching around the house and another (pointless?) visit to Huddersfield in the afternoon, unless I decided to have a walk round town first.

With a shock, the thought of town reminded me that I was due at Radio Haxford by half past ten in order to fulfil the eleven o'clock agony aunt slot. Leaving Cappy the Cat to his own devices, I rushed into the shower, dressed, and by ten, I was on my way out of the house. I didn't know what to expect, but maintaining some degree of normality, a routine which had been denied me since Friday evening, was vital under the circumstances, although how anyone could consider their radio debut to bear any resemblance to normality, I do not know.

I was dressed in my scruffs, a pair of old denims and a dark blue, woolly jumper. No one mentioned my attire when I entered the office, but then, Reggie had pointed out that it didn't matter on radio. He couldn't comment anyway. Wearing a tatty tracksuit and trainers falling off his feet, he was hardly a paradigm of sartorial elegance.

I accepted the commiserations of the staff on my current situation, and one of them spent time with me showing me how the system worked.

"All questions are monitored before the caller goes live, and before he or she is put through to you, the question appears on a small screen in front of you, with potential answers, giving you a little time to compose yourself. Just be cool, Mrs Capper, and you'll be fine."

At ten minutes to eleven, knees trembling just a little, I was ushered into the small studio, and sat opposite Reggie, making a determined effort to ignore his nose-wrinkling BO. I settled into my seat, familiarised myself with the layout, particularly the little, tablet-sized screen on which the questions would appear, and while Barry Manilow told us all about the events at the Copacabana, Reggie asked after Dennis and I brought him up to date on the situation so far.

"Outcome is still uncertain, Reggie, but we're clinging on to our hopes."

Diana Ross followed Manilow and at two minutes to the hour, with the final notes echoing through the headphones. Reggie went into his lead in.

"There you have it, people. Diana Ross telling us all about her Endless Love. You're listening to the Reggie Monk show on Radio Haxford, the station where it's all happening, brought to you by Haxford Breweries, the home of fine ales. If you must have a pint over the odds, make it a local brew. Ha-ha-ha. It's time for our weekly advice phone in, and this week we have a new lady in the hot seat, local vlogger, blogger and private eye, Christine Capper. Before we go any further, I must tell you that this lovely lady has suffered immense, personal trauma over the last few days after a cowardly attack on her husband, Dennis, senior partner at Haxford Fixers. The assault has left the poor man recovering in Huddersfield Royal, and our thoughts and prayers for a speedy recovery are with you, Dennis, and our sympathies go with you, Christine."

"Thank you, Reggie, and may I say a sincere thank you to all those Haxforders who sent messages of support over the weekend. Dennis and I and our whole family are touched by your kind thoughts."

As I spoke, the screen lit up with the first caller's question, and while Reggie led us into it, I studied the question and worked out my answer.

"Solidarity. That's how it is with your average Haxforder. On to our first caller, and she's Karen on line one. Good morning, Karen. You're live on the Reggie Monk show and what's your question for Christine."

"Good morning, Reggie. Before I ask you anything, Christine, can I offer my sympathies for what happened to your husband? I think you are very brave lady turning up on the radio after such a shocking event."

"Thank you, Karen. I'll pass on your message to my husband. Now, how can I help you?"

I was surprised at how calm I felt. It was as if the

weekend's traumatic events had left nothing for me to get anxious about, and I dealt with the first caller's question, quickly and easily, directing her to the Citizens Advice Bureau for detailed advice on how to deal with debt.

The second caller's question appeared as I concluded my first answer, and while Reggie once again led us into the call, I prepared my response. For the second time, the lady asking the question, offered condolences for our problems, before asking her question.

And so it went on for the whole fifteen minutes. Caller after caller, most of them women, asking for pointers on what were, for most Haxforders, common questions, mostly related to financial problems, and without exception, all offered their sympathies for my present situation.

To my relief, the forthcoming by-election was never mentioned.

At one minute past quarter past, Reggie brought the session to an end. "That's it for this morning's agony aunt spot, and I'm sure you will all want to join me in thanking Christine Capper. She'll be with you again at the same time next Tuesday. In the meantime let's hear from Lionel Ritchie who wants us all to know that she's Three Times a Lady. I'm sure he's talking about Christine."

As the music drifted in, Reggie closed down the on-air channel, and spoke to me alone. "You were absolutely top drawer, Chrissy. Turn it on like that every week and before you know it, you'll be taking over the whole morning programme from me. Ha-ha-ha."

I smiled. "I don't think I could leave Dennis for that long, Reggie. Thanks for having me."

"Ooh, that's a scurrilous allegation or I never heard one. Ha-ha-ha. See you next week, kiddo, and take my best wishes to Dennis. I hope he's on the mend real soon."

I came out of the studio into the office to a round of applause and handshakes from the staff. During the profusion of congratulation, I became aware that I was shaking. Retrograde nerves, I diagnosed. I hadn't had time to think about what I was doing while I was speaking to the callers, but now that it was over, the shakes had kicked in.

I noticed the telephone operators were busy, and the producer gave me the thumbs up. "Plenty of calls, Christine, most of them congratulating you on your sensible advice."

I had done it. I couldn't believe it, but I had done it. I had made my first appearance on local radio, and by the sounds of it, I was a success. It was time, I decided, to celebrate, and what better way than a toasted teacake and a cup of tea at Terry's?

Chapter Twenty-Two

Haxford market hall was large, but I was a frequent visitor and I knew every stall on every aisle. When I was fulfilling a large list of shopping, I could still get round the place in less than half an hour. This time, I swear it took me almost that long to get from Radio Haxford's upstairs office to Terry's Tea Bar, roughly in the centre of the hall.

I couldn't get more than a few paces before someone stopped me, commiserated on Dennis and congratulated me on my radio performance. By the time I finally got to Terry's, he had the teacake in the toaster, and a cup of tea waiting for me. As I handed over the money, he instructed me to sit down.

"Haxford's new megastar deserves personal service," he said.

Even while I was trying to eat and take in the enormity of the leap forward I had taken, people paused to commiserate and congratulate. And as I finished the teacake, a shadow fell over the table. My heart leapt and I looked up expecting to find Jorry accompanied by a couple of thugs.

It wasn't.

Holding a beaker of tea, Lizzie Finister looked as angry as she had the other day, but when she spoke, she was anything but annoyed. "May I join you?"

I said nothing but gestured at the seat opposite.

"I just heard you on the radio, and I have to say well done. You were cool, calm, and you sounded as if you were in control." She paused and sipped tea. "I was a bit peeved when we met last week. I'd just been sacked from Radio Haxford."

This time she waited for a comment. I kept my voice cold, unemotional. "You broke the golden rule of journalism, Lizzie. You took sides."

"I accept that, and I'm negotiating with Ian Noiland to end my suspension and get me back to work at the Recorder. I'll probably get a smack on the bottom, but I don't think he'll fire me."

"Good. I hope it works out for you." I took a wet of tea. "So was that all you wanted?"

"I've worked for the Recorder for a long time, and it's taught me a lot. The Haxford grapevine is the best in Yorkshire if not the country. Whisper is you had grief with Hal Jorry and a couple of his goons. Before they went after Dennis, I mean. And I'm truly sorry, Christine. Whether you and I see eye to eye is irrelevant. Dennis has worked on my car many times, and he's one of the best. He didn't deserve that."

"I'll make sure he knows when he regains consciousness… if he regains consciousness."

The irritation disappeared from her face, replaced by sadness. "Oh my God. I'm sorry. I didn't know it was that bad." She mirrored my actions and drank from her beaker. "Anyway, I was talking about the Haxford grapevine, and the whisper is you're looking into the death of that young kid on Thursday night. Wayne Pearson."

"Peason. Not Pearson."

"My bad. I don't know how far you've got, but I can tell you that I saw him in Jumping Jacks that night. He was well oiled and arguing with a woman, but Wayne stormed off. That was at about twenty past one in the morning. I mean, I'm not saying she had anything to do with what happened to him, but they were really at each other's throats. I'll tell you what was odd, though. The reports said he was walking home."

"I knew him, Lizzie. There's nothing odd about it. He was a waster, probably broke."

"That's just it. He wasn't. He hit on me earlier in the evening. I told him where to go, and in an effort to impress me, he offered to buy me a drink, and opened his wallet. He had a heck of a wedge in there, and they looked like twenties. He must have been carrying at least a grand. It was raining that night. Why would he walk home when he was loaded?"

It was logical and at the same time puzzling. "Did you see him leave?"

"Yes. Right after the argument with that woman. She wasn't far behind him, either. Again, I'm not saying she had anything to do with what happened but…" She trailed off, leaving the suggestion hanging in the air.

A slender thread began to spin out, leading me to an even thinner theory. "Can you describe this woman?"

"Not really. Plain, average looking, dark haired. Tell you what, I've an idea I've seen her somewhere, but I don't know where. Maybe on the checkouts in CutCost, but don't quote me on that."

"Thanks, Lizzie. I'll chase it up."

She finished her tea. "No problem. And again, I hope Dennis gets better soon."

She left me, and the stirrings of deep suspicion began to permeate, knitting together in my mind. I took out my phone and rang Mandy, asked if she could see me ASAP.

"Important?"

"The death of Wayne Peason."

"Come right over. We're busy with Singleton and Nesbitt, and going on what they're saying, I've already sent Sonny out to bring Jorry in. With a bit of luck, we'll have all three of them walled up by this afternoon."

I checked my watch. Just coming up to noon. "I'll be there in ten minutes."

Dominant amongst my jumbled emotions, suppressing my concerns for Dennis, smothering my worries for our future, was excitement. Neither Mandy nor Paddy would have considered it because they knew so little of the background, but I now knew what really happened on Thursday night/Friday morning, and the lies I had been told in an effort to bury it.

As always, Haxford made sure it took longer than ten minutes for the short journey from the market to the police station, and when I walked in, I had to suffer (if that's the right word) the sympathies of other officers, including Sergeant Vic Hillman, a man who wouldn't normally give me the time of day.

And when we got down to the nitty gritty, it wasn't just Mandy I faced, but her and Paddy, and they escorted me to an interview room, where Paddy took the lead.

"I heard about what happened with Jorry yesterday, Christine, and Mandy was out of order. She should have reported you for it. I've given her a private dressing down, and I'll do the same with you now. In the light of what happened to Dennis, I won't take any further action. Instead, I'll let it go with a verbal. Jorry deserves the boot up the backside, but not from you. You'll end up in more trouble than him. Understood?"

Coming from Paddy Quinn, that was mild. At any other time he would have torn me to shreds, and reported me for the incident.

I acquiesced. "Yes. And I'm sorry, Mr Quinn. It won't happen again."

"Good. Before we go any further, how's Dennis?"

I gave them a quick update on my husband's non-progress, then asked my first question. "The paint traces on Wayne's body. Have you identified them yet?"

They exchanged blank stares and it was Mandy who replied. "No. We're still waiting for the results."

"Check them against a ten year old Peugeot. I think you'll find a match. And if you can spare a couple of bodies to come with me, you can bring the perpetrator in. I know what it's about, I know who did it, and I know why."

More exchange of glances before Paddy

concentrated on me. "Well, don't keep it to yourself."

So I told them who and why, and I finished by insisting, "If you challenge her, she'll deny everything and you will struggle to prove it. If you let me hassle her in ways that you're not allowed to, I'll get to the truth."

Say what you like about Paddy Quinn, when it came to decisions, he had no trouble making them. "Go with her, Mandy. See what happens."

"Right, guv. What about Singleton, Nesbitt, and Jorry."

Paddy's familiar, sadistic smile came to his features. "Leave them to me. By the time you get back, I'll have 'em confessing to the Gunpowder Plot."

From the station, I followed the police cars to CutCost, and once we turned into the car park, with Mandy in the passenger seat of my Renault, they let me cruise ahead of them until I spotted the familiar Peugeot tucked up against the fence surrounding the vast parking area. As on the last time I saw it, she had nosed it in so that no one could see the front end without purposely walking round the car. Had it been reversed in, I would have spotted the damage on Friday, and my suspicions would have been roused then.

When we walked round the car and examined the bonnet, there was a large dent in the nearside wing and a cracked headlamp. It was similar to the damage to Jorry's Fiat, which had misled me the previous week.

Mandy, accompanied by Fliss Keele and Rehana

Suleman led the way into the store, and I tagged along. Once there, she spoke to Crompton, the assistant manager, the same man who had been about to sack John Frogshaw and Owen Trench before I stepped in, and a few minutes later, after he made a couple of calls, Janice Robertson was brought into a private office, where she sat facing Mandy and me, while Rehana and Fliss stood between her and the door, eliminating any possibility of running for it.

I didn't have time to wait for Janice trying to deny it all. I went straight on the attack. "I know you ran Wayne down, and I know why. The best thing you can do, Janice, is admit it."

Credit where it's due, she was as barefaced as the man himself. "I haven't a clue what you're talking about."

Mandy took over. "We've just examined your car and the damage to the front end. We got paint samples from Wayne's clothing, and it's only a matter of time before we match them to the paint job on your car. Do yourself a favour, Janice. Just tell us what it was all about."

She broke down and burst into tears. Rehana gave her a glass of water and when she had her emotions under some kind of control, she came back to us, her eyes pleading for understanding. "I didn't mean to kill him. I was just so mad at him when he got out of the car."

"Hold on, hold on," Mandy insisted. "Go back to the beginning."

Janice took a moment to compose herself. "I told Mrs Capper last week that he walked out on me, he left me virtually destitute, and the rotten sod took my car and sold it. I've been haggling since then to get the money off him, and he kept fobbing me off with one excuse after another. Then I met him on Thursday night in Jumping Jacks, and he was loaded. He had a good grand or more in his wallet. I hassled him, but he wouldn't hand over the money."

"That was the argument Lizzie Finister saw," I told Mandy.

"I followed him out of the club and the cheeky sod actually asked me for a lift home," Janice went on. "All that money, and he wouldn't even cough up for a taxi. Anyway, we got into my car, and as we were driving along, I gave him more earache, insisting I wanted my money. He eventually lost it, told me to stop the car and he'd walk the rest of the way. That was on Greenmount Lane. He walked off in front of me, and I saw my chance. If I could just clip him with the car, he'd be hurt, I could take the money, and I knew he'd never report it." Her face fell and she began to cry again. "I forgot he was drunk. As I drove at him, he staggered into the path of the car and I hit him too hard. He was still alive. I'm sure he was. I took the money out of his wallet, got into my car, and drove away. I was scared, and I swear he was alive. I didn't know he was dead otherwise I would've rung you there and then. As it was, I rang 999 from a call box on Batley Road, and then went home. When I read the story in the paper the next day, I was too frightened to come forward."

I believed her, and I'm sure Mandy did too, but it was time for her to formally caution the young woman, and then take her to the station.

I intervened. "Just a minute, Mandy. Janice, you say Wayne was carrying all this money. Did he say where he got it?"

"No. He wouldn't tell me. All he said was it came from a bloke he worked for years ago. He was a labourer for this guy, and as it always was with Wayne, he didn't stay there long. When did he ever?"

And with that, I had the solution to everything.

"Mandy," I said, "I know what's been going on, and I know exactly who is behind it all. If you let Rehana and Fliss take Janice to the station while you come with me, we can clear everything up in the next hour."

"Everything? You mean the blackmail business?"

"Yes. You might not get a prosecution out of it, but someone needs to read the riot act to this man, and it might as well be me and you."

Chapter Twenty-Three

A visit to Longberry Trading Estate told us that Keith McCrudden was at home, but Rowena Prune-face Benson refused to give us the home address until Mandy flashed her warrant card.

It was a grand and secluded house situated within sight of Castle Hill, a well-known, landmark in south Huddersfield, visible from most of the area. It could even be seen from the M62 if you knew where to look.

When Mandy announced us at the electronic gates, they opened, and we pulled into a large forecourt, where the McCruddens' limousine stood alongside a Mercedes saloon, the same one I'd seen outside the company offices on Thursday.

Eileen's chauffeur, presumably the general dogsbody too, opened the door and we barely had time to announce ourselves before he let us in.

Over the years, Dennis and I had stayed in many hotels, but the finest was in Paphos, Cyprus, which we visited for my fiftieth birthday. That hotel was four-star luxury, but it was a dosshouse at the side of the trappings in this mini-mansion.

The McCruddens were seated on two settees, facing each other, the furniture centred on a flash and fancy fireplace from which a coal-effect convector heater glowed. The room was comfortably warm, and it was a safe bet that they had no problems with the recent, scandalous rise in the price of gas.

Eileen was surprised to see us. "Christine, Sergeant Hiscoe. Is there something wrong? Only, I haven't received your bill yet."

"Because I haven't finished preparing it, Eileen, and yes there is something wrong, but I think it's up to your husband to tell you about it, not me."

If Keith McCrudden was put out by my challenge, he didn't show it. Instead, he looked down at his expensive, leather shoes for a moment, then looked up at me. "Nay, lass. It's better coming from you. I take it you know everything."

"The big picture, yes," I agreed, "but some of the details are a little hazy. Even so, I can hazard a guess at them. Wayne Peason worked for you years ago, didn't he?"

He appeared impressed. "How did you know?"

"My friend, Kim Aspinall, told me he'd done all sorts of jobs, even labouring on building sites, and when Janice Robertson told us he had a wallet full of money last Thursday, which he'd got from someone who once employed him as a labourer, I made the connection. He worked for you, and that was how he knew Eileen would be on that refresher course in Lancaster. And when you found out about him and your wife, you fired him. Didn't you?"

"I did. Wouldn't you if it was someone working for you and mixing it with your husband?"

I felt my anger rising. "My husband wouldn't get into that situation in the first place, Mr McCrudden, and talking of Dennis, do you know what happened to him? And it was your devious actions which were at the root of it."

He struggled to draw in a breath and let it out with a sigh. "You know something, when Eileen told me she was hiring a private eye, I wasn't bothered, and when I met you last Thursday, I was even less worried. To be honest, I didn't think you'd have the brains to work it all out. No offence intended."

"No, but plenty taken."

At this juncture, Eileen intervened. "Will someone please tell me what is going on?"

Keith left it to me and I was in no mood for pulling punches. "Someone sent copies of those incriminating letters to you, Eileen, and threatened to expose your, er, sexual proclivities. Let's call them that. That someone was Wayne Peason, but he didn't do it off his own bat. He did it because your husband paid him to do it. Wayne couldn't give a hoot whether you stood for election or not. If it had been him, he would have demanded money and even then there would be no guarantee he'd keep his mouth shut. Well, he got his money from your husband. And when I spoke to Keith on Thursday afternoon, he sent me on a wild goose chase after the other three candidates, Ambrose Davenport, Frederica Thornton, and Hal Jorry, and as a result of that, my husband was beaten up and is in hospital. His legs are broken, he has countless minor injuries, but worst of all his skull was fractured. He can't speak properly, he can't move, he doesn't know who he is, and he doesn't recognise me."

Throughout my necessary diatribe (necessary to expiate my fury) Keith could only look at the rich, shag-pile carpet, and Eileen's features went through what I believed was a well-rehearsed gamut from surprise, to shock to complete horror.

Keith looked up and at his wife. "I'm sorry, Eileen. I had to do it." Then he looked to me. "And I'm sorry for what happened to your old man, Christine. I will make the necessary restitution, and if he needs any extensive medical attention or disability aids, all you have to do is call and I'll arrange them."

"You think money will put this right?" I was losing my temper again.

Eileen's temper was getting the better of her, too, and she cut off her husband before he could respond to my challenge. "That doesn't explain the why, Keith."

Her husband suddenly looked much older than his sixty-six years. "I have my reasons, lass, which I'll get to in a minute." He took in both Mandy and me. "Everything got out of hand, but once I'd started it, I couldn't stop it. You're right, Christine. Finding Wayne Peason wasn't that difficult. He thought he was so smart, but a few questions here and there, and I tracked him down to that tatty bedsit. We met in a pub out on the moors. He was wary of me at first. He still remembered Eileen, still remembered how I booted him out when I found out about their fling. I brought him round with a couple of beers, and put the proposition to him. Eileen still had those disgusting letters he'd written to her and copies of the ones she'd sent to him. Our arrangement was he would photograph them and send them to her phone and her email from an anonymous address, which he did... for a price. Crikey, I've never seen anyone negotiate like him. I can be tough when I'm haggling, but he left me at the starting gate. In the end, we agreed on five grand, two and a half up front, the rest when Eileen stepped down. Then you went to see him on Thursday before you came to see me. He actually rang me in a panic before you got to my place. I was expecting you, and that gave me time to think of a diversion." Like Janice Robertson, he turned to pleading. "I promise you, I didn't know Jorry was going to run him down, and I didn't know he was going to beat up your husband, or I'd never have tipped him off or sent you to him."

Mandy chipped in. "You're wrong on at least one of those counts, Mr McCrudden. Jorry may well have had a hand in beating up Mr Capper, but he had nothing to do with running Wayne Peason down. We arrested the guilty party an hour ago, and she – note gender – has already made a full confession. My colleagues will be taking a formal statement and she'll be charged later this afternoon. It remains to be seen, sir, whether you're guilty of anything other than incitement to blackmail, and that would depend upon your wife pressing charges against you. Personally, I'd hang you out to dry, but it's not my decision."

A stiff silence fell for a moment. It was Eileen who broke it. Her face was aghast, a study in shock at the things she had learned. "Why, Keith? Why did you want me to withdraw after all the work I've put in on my campaign? Parliament has been my life's ambition, and you know it, so why?"

He turned away, unable to look at her.

Thoughts of Dennis filled my mind, and I felt no sympathy for him, but I knew that if I didn't say something, he wouldn't, and whatever had or hadn't happened, Eileen deserved the truth. "I think I can answer that, Eileen. He needs you here, at home, not swanning around Westminster. Isn't that right, Keith?"

He gave the barest of nods.

"His health is failing," I went on. "I noticed it the first time we met. A coughing fit and he turned almost purple. What is it, Keith? Asthma? COPD? Lung cancer?"

"The big C." He sucked in as deep a breath as he could. "They say they can operate, but they don't know how far it's spread." He appealed to his wife again. "I'm sorry, Eileen. I didn't know how to tell you. Like Christine said, I need you here, not yattering in Westminster, and I didn't know how to stop you without wrecking what we had. No matter what ups and downs we've gone through, you've been the best of all possible wives."

It didn't surprise me when she moved across the room to sit with him, took his hand and then hugged him. I felt quite choked and Mandy could only look the other way. She was a stranger to close relationships, which struck me as absurd considering the size of her bump. I mean, how much closer could a couple get?

At length, Eileen let go of her husband, and faced me. "Christine, we owe you a huge apology, you and your husband. Send me your final account, and I'll ensure it's paid immediately. Beyond that, as Keith has already said, let me know exactly what Dennis needs, and I'll make sure he gets it. I'm sorry for all the trouble we've caused, Sergeant. If there are any charges to follow, we will plead guilty without argument. Now, if you'll excuse me, it's time I put aside my personal ambitions, and sorted out my husband's care."

Epilogue

That concludes the whole, sorry and sordid story. It seemed incredible that one woman's ten-year-old misdemeanour could come back to haunt her and create so many problems for others, not least me and my husband, and I have to say that if her husband had employed the same candour, the same, basic honesty with her as he did with others, none of this would have happened.

The shaven haired thug, Bernard Singleton, was found to have a cut and bruise on one ankle, caused when Dennis lashed out with the piece of piping he'd been holding. My husband was a strong man, and the blow was enough to draw blood, some of which remained on the pipe and was enough to help convict Singleton. Mandy had described the two men as 'berks' and it was accurate. When Nesbitt's unregistered mobile was checked, he hadn't even bothered to erase the photograph of Dennis and the follow up message they'd sent to me. Unwilling to take full responsibility, Singleton testified against Nesbitt, and Nesbitt testified against Singleton, and both of them testified that Hal Jorry had paid them to carry out the attacks on me and my husband. All three received lengthy prison sentences for their despicable activities.

Janice Robertson pleaded guilty to involuntary manslaughter, and she, too, was jailed, but for a shorter sentence than the thugs who almost killed my husband and decimated my life.

In withdrawing from the by-election, Eileen McCrudden went public on her indiscretion and her husband's condition, and I'm sure that everyone in Haxford now knows that Ambrose Davenport was elected to replace Cyril Utterridge.

Dennis was eventually discharged after a three-week stay in Huddersfield Royal, but he was nothing like the man he used to be. He could not walk. His bones were mending, but he had a long way to go before he would stand on his own two feet, and for the time being, he was confined to a wheelchair. He could not speak properly, and his memory worked in fits and starts. There were times when he did not recognise me, times when he did. When Simon and I got him home, he did not know the house, and although he cuddled Cappy the Cat (who responded with a warning hiss and an open-clawed determination to escape Dennis's unwanted attention) he did not know our moggie's name. Neither did he recognise Simon, Naomi or Bethany, and Ingrid was a complete stranger to him when she paid us a flying visit. I took him to the workshop, where Tony, Lester and Geoff made a fuss of him, but he knew none of them, and the same was true of Sandra when we made our way up to the Snacky, where she supplied food and drink, and sat with us for half an hour.

The McCruddens were as good as their word. Within a few days of Dennis's discharge from hospital, a nearly new Fiat Diablo people carrier arrived, complete with a slide-out ramp at the rear, and inside was a powered wheelchair. Dennis hated Fiats and it would be interesting to see what he made of it when he was fully recovered… if that happy day ever arrived. Eileen rang, and after accepting my gratitude for the vehicle, said that once Dennis was ready for physiotherapy, I had to get in touch with her, and she would arrange it with a private practitioner.

With the help of Tony Wharrier and Geoff Vetch, Dennis's replacement at Haxford Fixers, I managed to sell my ageing and trusty Renault, and it was with a feeling of sadness that I watched it driven away one sunny morning towards the end of May.

After a month of Tuesday morning slots, Radio Haxford told me that listening figures had not increased, but on the plus side, they had not gone down either, and the general consensus was that I was doing a good enough job in the agony aunt sessions.

The case of blackmail at the ballot box, proved to be a huge learning curve for me. After so many years married, I took our comfortable life for granted. Now, it was anything but comfortable. Dennis needed constant attention, and aside from the medical issues, I was the only one who could provide his personal and pastoral care. It was hard work. Much harder than I'd had to work at any other time in my life. Naomi helped where and when she could, but with the best will in the world, she had a young child to deal with, so most of the time, everything fell to me.

We had to get the builders in to alter access to the house, install wheelchair ramps at the side door and the conservatory, and that put paid to my plans for a refurbished kitchen.

If the case taught me anything, it was summarised by something Dennis said to me when we were in Sandra's Snacky the day before Singleton and Nesbitt attacked him. When it comes to politics and politicians, give it a wide berth. I don't think he said it in those precise words, but that was his meaning, and if I had a low opinion of politicians before the case, it sank even lower.

And on that note, I'll bid you good day. Tune in next week to Christine Capper's Comings & Goings, when I'll have more tales from Haxford and the surrounding area.

THE END

The Author

David W Robinson retired from the rat race after the other rats objected to his participation, and he now lives with his long-suffering wife in sight of the Pennine Moors outside Manchester.

Best known as the creator of the light-hearted **Sanford 3rd Age Club Mysteries**, and in the same vein, the brand new series, **Mrs Capper's Casebook**. He also produces darker, more psychological crime thrillers; the **Feyer & Drake** thrillers and occasional standalone titles.

He, produces his own videos, and can frequently be heard grumbling against the world on Facebook at **https://www.facebook.com/dwrobinson3** and has a YouTube channel at **https://www.youtube.com/user/Dwrob96/videos**. For more information you can track him down at **www.dwrob.com**

By the same author

(All titles are exclusive to Amazon)

Self-Published works

Mrs Capper's Casebooks
Mrs Capper's Christmas
Death at the Wool Fair
Blackmail at the Ballot Box
A Professional Dilemma

Titles published and managed by Darkstroke Books

The Sanford 3rd Age Club Mysteries
The Filey Connection
The I-spy Murders
A Halloween Homicide
A Murder for Christmas
Murder at the Murder Mystery Weekend
My Deadly Valentine
The Chocolate Egg Murders
The Summer Wedding Murder
Costa del Murder
Christmas Crackers
Death in Distribution
A Killing in the Family
A Theatrical Murder
Trial by Fire
Peril in Palmanova
The Squires Lodge Murders
Murder at the Treasure Hunt
A Cornish Killing

Merry Murders Everyone
Tales from the Lazy Luncheonette Casebook
A Tangle in Tenerife
Tis the Season to Be Murdered
Confusion in Cleethorpes
Murder on the Movie Set
A Deadly Twixmas

The Midthorpe Mysteries
Missing on Midthorpe
Bloodshed in Benidorm

Feyer & Drake
The Anagramist
The Frame

Standalone titles
The Cutter
Kracht

THANK YOU FOR READING. I HOPE YOU HAVE ENJOYED THIS BOOK. IF SO IT WOULD BE WONDERFUL IF YOU COULD LEAVE A REVIEW ON AMAZON?

Printed in Great Britain
by Amazon

34161332R00129